WEREWOLF IN SHINING ARMOR

WOLF KNIGHTS
BOOK ONE

MINERVA HOWE

For Alex, Jason, Jaymi, Michael, and my Patreon crew, who make me look better than I am.

To the D&D group who came up with the idea.

To all the werewolf fans, who keep after me to remember the non-dragon stories. And, as always, to my wife BA.

CHAPTER

ONE

Inner peace.

That was what he told himself. He could find it. Symon knew he could.

Inner peace.

Calm.

Emptiness.

Symon took a deep breath in, held it, and let it out nice and slow, making a sound as he released.

Ooohm.

His yoga mat lay solid beneath him, the air just barely warming from the deep night chill, and the scent of sandalwood incense drifted through the air, faint and sweet.

At this time in the early morning, when his Boulder courtyard was quiet and full of peace, it was just what he needed. The birds chirped and sang, and the wind chimes tinkled gently as the breeze blew down off the Rockies and onto the front range. It was blissful as it guided him. Allowing him to move to the next stage of being.

Drop him deeper into his meditation.

If his brothers heard him thinking, they would put Nair in his shampoo bottle. No question.

They both thought he was too controlled. Too out of touch with his nature.

Ooohm.

He needed to center, and he absolutely did not need to think about his wild brothers. Not today.

Today, he started his new position as the CEO at Shiftr.com, the holding company for the best shifter apps out there.

It wasn't as if he'd gone in guns blazing, Mr. Hostile Takeover Man or anything, but...well, he'd wanted the company, and when push had come to shove, the bunny shifter that had founded the dot.com?

Had wanted to sail around the world on his personal yacht way more than he'd wanted to fight with Symon. Hell, Symon thought he hadn't wanted to fight with anyone.

Now he had the company he wanted, but he wasn't 100 percent sure that he knew what to do with it. What he did know was that all of the employees at the company were worried about a wolf taking over the top executive's position. As far as they were concerned, he wasn't techie, he wasn't smart enough to be one of them, and he didn't have what it took to run this company. He was just a wolf shifter. A slavering beast.

He was going to prove them wrong.

Immediately if not sooner.

Ooohm.

Focus, for fuck's sake.

Symon spent hours meditating every morning, doing one asana after another. It was supposed to remind him that he was not some feral creature. He was not a wolf at the whim of the moon. He was not apt to bite and claw and spread his scent.

He was a sophisticated, controlled being.

He'd spend his entire life fighting—his brothers, his family, his pack. They wanted him to be some sort of... lumberjack up in the tree line, making dozens of babies and running with the moon.

He didn't even own any flannel.

Ooohm.

Tink.

Woosh.

Click.

Clink.

The sounds started slowly, gently, but soon Symon could hear movement in the house behind him. He didn't tense—he didn't have to. Stan had been with him for decades, and he presented no danger to Symon.

Symon had been on a run on the day before the full moon, and he'd come across a man wounded during a vicious attack.

A werewolf attack that had horrified him, and it had made him commit to never letting the wolf take him again. He'd stayed with Stan, had helped him heal and adjust to his new life as an infected human. And now Stan had a place with him as long as he needed it. For life.

While he didn't have the slightest idea who had attacked Stan, he had guilt, and Stan had needed a place to stay where he could safely live out his life span without having to go outside.

It worked out perfectly, because Symon had needed someone to take care of the basics for him. Food, cleaning, emails—things that he didn't want to take care of. It was a mutually beneficial relationship, and they both managed to live together quite easily. They were like ships that passed in the night.

It didn't hurt that his house was huge and that Stan had his own wing that had complete privacy, of course.

At any rate, the little noises meant that coffee would appear, the scent making his nose twitch, and soon there would be an omelet.

Given that today was Monday, it would have ham. Ham and peppers, onions, and cheese. Tomorrow's breakfast would be pancakes and bacon. Wednesday would be oatmeal, Thursday potato and egg breakfast tacos, and Friday was biscuits and sausage gravy.

On Saturdays, he made himself a peanut butter and banana sandwich, while on Sundays he took himself to brunch in Boulder, if he was in town.

Stan was nothing if not predictable.

A butterfly landed on his nose, startling him. That was unexpected, and he didn't ever know what to do with that. Blow it off? Eat it? Study its beauty?

Ooohm.

He and Stan did have their rhythm going on here. He meditated. He practiced yoga. He bought companies that he was curious about and learned how they ticked. Stan woke up, made coffee and freshly pressed orange juice, then started breakfast before disappearing to surf all the news outlets and watch hours of Real Lycans of New York.

He had a rhythm of his own.

Soon Symon would go in and take his shower.

Get dressed for the day.

Wolf down his breakfast—pun absolutely intended.

Grab his to-go cup of coffee and his phone. And head out the door.

Normal.

Reasonable.

Comfortable. No matter what job he was working, even a new one.

Tonight, he would have supper at his men's club. Friday night. He would take in a play. Or show in Denver. On the weekends, he would go farther up into the mountains, sometimes camp. Oftentimes just walk along in nature completely clothed, non furry, nonthreateningly. He even slept in a tent. No wild nature for him. It tempted him to wolf out.

Ooohm.

Unlike his idiot brothers, he did not feel the need to hunt.

Or to stalk or to run around wearing nothing but a tail and teeth. He felt no urge to bathe under the moon.

That sort of nonsense was what gave all of them bad names.

Of all of the various shifters who existed in the world, Symon failed to understand why his kind, the wolves, were so widely considered savages, lost to the wiles of the moon.

No one ever said, oh, those bears, they're going to bite you. Or, why don't we muzzle those cats? Or even, those were bison. They're just so dangerous.

He didn't think anyone was aware of how many people were harmed by werebuffalo in any given year. The numbers were shocking.

Or what about deer? They ran into cars. They ran through windows. They were completely and utterly as apt to get into trouble as werewolves were.

And that didn't even begin to cover the sharks. Those guys liked to bite people for fun and profit.

Ooohm.

He forced his mind back into the middle.

Right. Focus.

Work.

Business.

This was what he was good at, what he needed to make his point. This was why he had taken this company over.

He was going to prove to everyone that werewolves could be logical, reasonable creatures who could live in complete sophistication.

Debonair, even.

Shiftr.com was the shifter community's most up-and-coming social media platform. It allowed lycans of all types to meet one another online, to join together and get to know one another in a safe and nonthreatening space.

The original programming had been rough, sloppy, but in the last few years, there had been someone in the company who worked their butts off to speed it up, to make it classier.

Symon wasn't sure which one of the employees, or which *ones* of the employees for that matter were responsible for this, but he was going to find out and he was going to reward them.

The building was on the outskirts of Denver on the Boulder side, and so he felt comfortable driving out there to the glass-and-steel building while still being able to come home every day to his home near the mountains.

Surely between his new position in the company and being this close to Denver, he would be able to make the right decisions. Prove what he'd been telling his brothers for years.

All he had to do was move into the circles wherein those in the know could meet him, come to know him, understand that yes, he was a businessman and yes, he was very shrewd and sharp about what he did, but he did nothing that was not logical and practical and calculated. He was not at the whim of the moon.

Ooohm.

His nose twitched at the smell of the ham, which was caramelizing so well that it made his mouth water. Dammit, he wasn't done meditating. He needed to tell Stan to back breakfast off five more minutes every day. He couldn't concentrate with the smell of—

No. He could. He could. He finished his freaking meditation without breaking for food. That was what willpower was about. Denied gratification.

To his credit, Stan waited for Symon to walk inside, even though Symon knew the man hated for his food to get cold.

"Coffee?" Stan's tone radiated disapproval.

"Yes, thank you. Though make it to go. I'll eat and run today."

"Oh, but—"

"Thank you, Stan." He took the coffee and the omelet plate that Stan handed him.

"Good fortune today, sir."

"Thank you, but I won't need fortune, Stan. I'm prepared."

"Of course you are. I would, erm, shower quickly after you eat."

Symon resisted the urge to sniff his pit. "Yes, well. I probably will."

Stan left him, and he groaned. What was he giving away to every other shifter in the entire business at this rate? Goddess. His nerves vibrated, making him grit his teeth. He could do this. He was going to do this.

Half an hour later, he was on his way into the city, the miles flying by. He hated the traffic and the smog that hung over the city on some days. Most shifters chafed at that, no matter what kind they were.

He strode into the office five minutes before the start of his workday, signing in with the security guard.

"Good morning, sir."

"Morning, Manny. How's your wife?" The man's wife had just given birth last week.

"Very well, thank you for asking."

"Good, good." He held his keycard to the executive elevator door call sensor. "Have a good one."

"You too. And they're loaded for bear up there, sir."

"Mmm." Too bad they were getting a wolf. The joke made him wince even as it made a smile curve his lips.

Then he quashed it. Controlled. Calm.

Ooohm.

The executives he could handle. It was getting the respect of the employees who created the vision of the company. Those were the people he needed to get on board. He needed to establish a rapport with them so he could help guide them in a direction that satisfied both them and the board.

As he walked into the executive suite, he scanned the faces there, all of them waiting for him. He knew none of them were his fans. Not yet.

"Good morning, everyone. I'll be taking an hour to meet with my new assistant and get accustomed to my office and look at my schedule. After that, I have a mixer meeting scheduled for the rest of the company to attend. They may come and go as they please, but I strongly suggest that you encourage all of the people in your departments to attend." He waited a few beats for them to disperse and fought a growl. "Well, go!"

They went, but he felt defeated by the wolf coming to the fore.

He'd better get his shit together.

He had a lot of people to meet.

＊

"ADRIAN, I need you to go to the damn meet-and-greet."

Adrian Blaidd blew out a sharp breath. "I don't want to. I have this algorithm almost—"

His boss, Helene, clicked her nails on his desk to get his attention, which of course, did. She had long acrylic nails. "Adrian. I have been ordered by the new CEO to make certain all my people attend. I have no doubt the big jerk is having the cameras in all the areas watched." Helene was a fox shifter who was sleek, darkly ginger, and wily. She could also bite. Hard.

And god help a guy if she screamed at him. Time literally stopped.

"But why does he need to meet me?" Adrian hoped he wasn't being...well, what? Whiny? He was serious about his job. He was good at tech stuff. But not socializing, especially with the brass. And this was the big wig.

Not to mention another wolf.

No. He would stay in his office.

"He wants to meet everyone. You're one of the many. You go in, you have a cookie, you leave. Easy-peasy." She bared her sharp little teeth. "Say 'Yes, Helene'."

"Mmhmm...yes, Helene." Not happening. "I'll be there."

Not.

"I will dock you if you aren't, Adrian. I mean it." She glared, her expression somehow knowing. She had his number. He adored her. She was the best manager he'd ever had. But this sucked.

He'd moved to Denver because he was his own wolf, not just some omega on the low end of the totem pole.

The last rung of the omega chain?

Whatever.

He fucking *rocked*.

You are smart. Sexy. Smart. Also, really good at your job. Right? Right.

But now this new CEO had moved in, and he seemed to be pushing the pack structure in the company. Adrian wanted nothing to do with that.

Nope.

He was a lone wolf. Did his own shit. Was solitary, and—

Why was Helene still standing there?

"What?"

"Come on. Let's go have a little coffee and convo."

"Oh, god." He rolled his eyes. "Evil woman."

"I know. I do, but you're so tense, and I know how you are. You'll scamper out of here and not get things done."

"Scamper?" He did not scamper.

"Come with me. Ten minutes. Then you can come back to work." She grabbed his arm and dragged him toward the elevator.

Wow, she was strong.

"So, what about the new guy? Decent? Freaky?"

"Mmm. Well, he's very controlled." She grinned a little. "But he seems interested in the company and not just the money."

"That's good, I guess?" He was going to miss bouncy little Adam, if he was honest.

"I suppose, yes. It might be bad for some of us middle management," she said wryly. "I bet he cuts deadwood."

"You're not deadwood, lady! You're an amazing manager. I swear." He loved working for her.

"Maybe he'll get rid of Dave."

"Yeah." Adrian wrinkled his nose. No one liked Dave, and no one could really understand what he did at the company.

Werecrocodiles were so...challenging.

"Wow, look at that spread." They walked into the big conference area, where a brunch buffet was laid out. There was a waffle bar.

That had to have cost a fortune.

"Is it real maple syrup?"

He reacted poorly to sugar substitutes.

"It is." The attendant smiled. "There's other kinds as well, but apparently the new owner likes the good things in life."

"Huh." Well, then. Waffles ahoy. He could take them to his desk.

He piled up his plate, ducking his head as one of the male mountain lions came stalking by, the big asshole trying to cut in line.

"Hey!" Helene stepped in, almost chest bumping the guy. "Line starts back there, Carl."

"Sure." Carl lifted his lip, a snarl so evident.

"Asshole. Okay, kiddo. Please eat at least a bite of that here." Helene grabbed a waffle and about a dozen pieces of bacon.

"Okay. I will. I promise." He found a standing table next to the door that was totally empty and ate a bite of bacon.

Isaac came wandering close. "Can I share with you, please?"

The Pallas cat's expression was a perpetual scowl, but Isaac was the head of the mail room, and an incredibly focused, organized, and kind man.

"Of course. It's nice and quiet over here."

"Yes. And no big jerks." Isaac made a rough kitty coughing sound. "Really what does it take for them to just mind their own business?"

"Is someone bothering you, Isaac?" He could speak to Helene. Being the only department head who was an omega made it tough for Isaac sometimes.

"No one I can't handle." Isaac looked at his fork. "Crab cakes. Can you believe it? At a work buffet. In Denver." He chomped his in one huge bite.

His sweet tooth made those waffles taste like heaven, and he powered through the stack. He wasn't a cook, so he didn't eat well at home.

That was...wow. And he didn't start to feel sick right away, either, so the syrup was good. They didn't need to chitchat a lot, him and Isaac. They just stood there and chowed down on their food.

"I'm going back in. Want anything else."

"Mmm. A cinnamon roll?" He would take that to go.

"I'll get you sweets." Isaac was a salty fishy guy.

"Thank you. You rock."

Isaac winked at him, then slowly wandered up toward the front.

He saw it, Carl's foot swinging out to knock Isaac over.

His wolf roared to the forefront, and he rushed over to make sure Isaac didn't fall.

"Jesus, you fucker!"

"What did you call me?" Carl whirled on him, moving so fast, turning on him as he caught Isaac mid-stumble.

"You heard me? What are you, twelve? This is an office! You don't trip people, you giant bully."

"I will rip your throat out, pup."

There was precious little doubt of that, but he wasn't a coward. "Again. Work. Back off."

Isaac hissed. "Go away, dickhead."

Carl scowled, raising a hand, and he pushed Isaac behind him, stepping up to ward off whatever punch the big fucker was going to throw.

"That's enough!" Someone whizzed right past him, taking up a huge amount of space between him and Carl, looming over the big cat shifter. "You don't threaten people in this company. Do you understand? You're on suspension."

"Whaaat?" Carl's voice rose with surprise. "Over these snivelly omegas?"

"I am not snivelly!"

"Yeah!" Isaac leaned around him to sneer at Carl.

"Out. I'll speak to you at your disciplinary meeting." The guy who'd moved between him and Carl waited, and Carl slunk off.

The man turned to face him, and he had time to register two things. This was the new boss, and he was incredibly, shockingly, distressingly hot, with a wing of raven black hair and bright amber eyes.

"Are you all right?"

"Of course." Adrian tried to step back, but his heel hit Isaac's foot. The kitty grunted, staggering into him, and Adrian turned, reaching out to grasp the table next to him for balance. A plate went flying into the air, and he wanted to die as the contents splattered the new boss's expensive suit.

His eyes went wide. "Oh god. Oh god. Oh god."

Someone gasped, "Club soda?"

Isaac handed over a mostly finished glass of Sprite. "What? It's close."

His wolf was running in hysterical circles in his mind, utterly panicked.

"No, thank you. I'll just have it cleaned." The boss smiled faintly. "I know you're Isaac, but who might you be?"

"Nobody. Just a worker bee. I'm sorry. I didn't mean to—"

"Adrian! What on earth happened?" Helene came running. "Go on to the bathroom and get yourself cleaned up. Work virtual for the rest of the day."

"'kay." He turned and ran for the stairway. His laptop was at home, his wallet and keys were in his pocket. He'd wash out his coffee cup when he got in next.

Well. At least he guessed the boss knew now that he'd been at the welcome meeting, right?

CHAPTER

TWO

What a fucking disaster. As first days stood, this one was probably the worst one Symon had encountered in his entire career.

He took the glass of wine Stan had poured for him as a pre-dinner relaxation technique and walked to the big picture window in the living area. He stared out at the mountains, a muscle jumping in his jaw.

He'd ruined a suit. Fired a mid-level manager who was no doubt going to cause trouble. And he'd met the most... fascinating omega he'd ever seen.

His phone rang, and he knew before he answered it who it was.

Rian.

He didn't even have to guess.

"Hello, brother."

"Sy," Rian growled, "Quincy says you had a terrible day."

"Quincy is an—" uncanny son of a bitch "—asshole."

"Bah. He wanted me to check on you."

"Why didn't he call me himself?"

15

Rian chuckled, the sound like rusty gates opening. "Because he only gets one phone call, and I am the lawyer in the family?"

"Wait, what?" Quincy was in jail? "What the hell happened now?"

"Another fight. He apparently jumped over the bar and beat a man with a baseball bat for hitting an omega. He takes it personal."

"He'll have a way harder time in jail," Symon pointed out. "Omegas tend to."

Rian snorted. "One, I dare anyone. Two, he has your money and my brilliance. It's never going to happen."

"Yeah, yeah. This is just what I needed today, bro." His brothers made him nuts. Like going to the nuthatch nuts.

"Oh, don't worry about Quin. He's a turd, but he knows his business." Rian didn't sound worried. "What about you?"

"I know my business."

"That's not what I mean." Rian sighed dramatically. "Why are you having a shit day?"

He thought about just denying it all. But then he decided better to lay it on Rian than to bust out with something wolfy tomorrow at work. "First day was shit. Fired a manager for being a fucking bully. One of the bullied spilled an entire plate of food on my favorite suit—"

"The gray silk?" Rian yelped. He shared Symon's fashion sense.

"Yes! I have it at the cleaners, but—"

"Oh, that is a travesty. Did you bite him, because that would be unfortunate."

"No. No, it wasn't his fault. And he's..." Adorable. Sweet. Utterly confusing.

"Well, good. Not about the suit, of course, but the lack

of biting. So, the new business, are you going to make it wildly successful for us?"

"I am. And I want it to innovate the whole scene." Shifters needed to be able to feel secure. Dating was just a good place to start.

"Good deal. You let me know what you need from me. You want me to come growl at your mean manager? I know you don't love growling in public."

"No, he's gone. Though he's a mean-spirited ass. In fact, at least half the middle management at this company are fuckheads, which is not too surprising. The owner who sold to us was a pushover. Nice. Techie. He's now designing the next app we'll buy while he yachts around the world."

"Yes, his lawyer was an ostrich. She wanted to have a torrid affair."

"With you?" Rian and an ostrich. The picture made him snort. Then chuckle. Then laugh right out loud.

"I know!" Rian's laughter made him chortle. "Can you imagine? Me and a dirty little bird? She wasn't going to be able to handle what I have to offer."

"No. Not unless you wanted her to bite you. Those birds can do damage."

"No shit. She was...vexed."

"Oh, damn." That sent him off again, gales of laughter ripping him.

They might make him nuts, but they both could, in their own ways, make him happy.

"Anyway, you're going to be fine," Rian told him finally. "You know it. Get the worst day over at the first, and boom. The rest is gravy."

"Mmm."

"Gravy."

They laughed again, but he sobered quickly. "Take care of Quin, huh?"

"I will."

"Take money out of the shared account. As much as you need."

"I will. I think I have an angle where I can get the guy to drop the charges."

"You are the best lawyer on earth."

"I know. Lunch a week from Thursday?"

"Text Stan. Tell him to put it on my schedule."

"You do it. Love you, Sy. Ciao."

"Love you, bye."

When they hung up, he drank down the rest of his wine, then called out to Stan. "Going to take a shower before supper." He'd changed at work, so now he wanted to get clean.

And if he relaxed himself enough to enjoy supper by jacking off to that worried little omega? Then so be it.

Are you okay?

HE WAS IN HIS SWEATPANTS, in the dark, a box of pizza next to him on the sofa. He had a Coke and some reality show on TV, his laptop and an order from Insomnia cookies on the way.

He was fucking fabulous.

Fine, Isaac. You all right?

Yeah. Carl got fired.

His eyes widened when he saw the text.

Whaaaat?

What the hell? Carl had been deeply entrenched in management.

True fucking story. Like walked out by security fired. Can you believe it?

NO!

Oh, that was pretty damn cool. Carl was an asshole. He was surprised. The man was one hell of a salesperson and had gotten away with shit for years.

Yep. He had a meeting with the new boss, and apparently he threatened the guy

Isaac sent all kinds of emojis about mirth.

I got nothing. That is just wild, man.

A single cat could take down a wolf, even a strong one.

Well, as long as you're cool

Isaac sent a little ice cube image.

Yeah.

Goddess, no.

He was going to have to work hard to never, ever be in the presence of that wolf again. Never. He was—intense. Sexual. Wolfy. Adrian would probably dream about him. But he didn't need that in his life.

He was a lone wolf, dammit.

Want to play?

They had a few first-person shooters that they played together, and lord knew he didn't want to work.

Fuck yeah.

Cool. Let's do it.

They picked a game, and he grabbed his controller, joining in immediately. This was simple. Easy. And it kept him from thinking.

He sighed softly, rolled his shoulders. He needed to get his shit together. He loved his job. Shiftr.com was to the lycan community as Facebook, Tindr, and Instagram was to the humans.

He'd been working with his team for months to rework the code to make the interface faster, easier, more logical. More end-user friendly. And they were doing amazing things.

Why they had to sell out now...

Rabbits were too easy to freak out. Seriously. Not cool.

He was just going to have to suck it up and—

His phone rang, making him jump a foot off the couch. He landed hard and looked at the phone, but he didn't know the number. It was work related, though, because it just said Shiftr Inc. on the caller info.

"Dammit." He picked up with a frown. "'lo?"

"Adrian Blaidd?"

"This is he. Who is this?" He never just said yes. He was in tech; he knew better.

"This is Symon Lukos. I'm sorry to call after work hours, but it took a while for my new assistant to get me your phone number."

"Oh. I…" Fuck, he was fired, wasn't he? "I'm so sorry about your suit. Honest."

"No, no. Don't worry about it. I just wanted to make sure you were all right. I don't tolerate the sort of behavior you endured today."

"I—I couldn't let anyone hurt Isaac. He's little."

"He is. I appreciate your initiative. I will call him as well. But I wanted to let you know, I looked into what your team is doing, and I'm very impressed."

"You are?" Oh. Oh, thank the moon. "We love what we do, you know? We really do."

Not fired. So not fired.

"I can tell. The interface is so much smoother with this rollout."

Wow. That was more tech speak than he'd expected from the new boss, too, and he warmed to it. "We worked hard on the flow. And the algorithms. We wanted people to be able to see what they want, not just random posts."

"That's obvious. I've spent a long time with the software, putting it through its paces."

"That's cool. I mean, I'm really glad." Shit, he just needed to shut up. He was about to say that his old boss had written the original software and then just kind of stopped caring. But that was trash talk, and not professional. "We love it. Please don't shut it down."

Oh fuck.

Shut up.

"I have no intention of it. I think we can expand it without bloating it. And hone it in at the same time."

"Good. Good. I know I have lots of ideas. Lots of them." He bounced a little on the sofa. "I meant, my manager does."

"Helene is in no danger, Adrian. I promise. She's a good manager and a shrewd businessperson."

"Oh. Good." Whew. "Well, I really appreciate it. She rocks, and she's great to work for."

> Dude, are you okay?

> Fine. THE BOSS IS CALLING ME

> Helene?

> The new guy

He didn't even remember the guy's name... Symon?

> Holy shitballs. Are you fired?

> No.

"At any rate, thank you for your hard work and your bravery."

"Sure." What else did he say?

"Good night, Adrian." Something about the way the boss said his name made him shiver.

"Um. Night."

Whoa.

Whoa, that was...

A little perverse, if he was honest.

He texted Isaac one more time.

> He's calling you next. I'm gonna go take a shower.

> OMG. Calling me? I'm logging off. BYE!

> Bye

He put his controller away and took the pizza leftovers to the fridge. Cookies. Hmm. He should wait for them to—

The doorbell rang, and he laughed. Right. Cookies, then a shower. A guy had to have priorities.

THREE

"I don't care who he was fucking, he's not coming back." Symon was sick of dealing with this shit. Whoever this Carl guy was, he must be holding something over the heads of half the management. This was the third day in a row some jerk had made an impassioned plea for him to be re-hired.

"Well, I never!"

He bit back the snarl and the, "Yep, that's your problem," that wanted to snap out. That was unprofessional of him. So he crossed his arms, leaned against his desk, and stared. Hard. Without speaking.

"I quit."

"All right." He grabbed his phone. "Laurel, have security escort—" He glanced at the furious man before him. "What is your name again?"

"Henry Gaines."

"Henry Gaines to his desk to get his things. Only his, please." A guy who would be in league with Carl would probably not be above pinching a few things here and there.

"Yes, sir."

He hung up. "I wish you luck."

The guy sputtered but left with security when they came, and he blew out a frustrated breath. Then he called his assistant. "I need Helene Jamis up here, please."

"Of course, sir. I'm on it." That happy voice proved to him that he'd made the right decision. Someone liked Helene a lot more than the late, unlamented Henry Gaines.

It was a damn minefield, this taking over an established company. This wasn't the first time he'd done it, but it was his first tech company, where it wasn't just sales at stake, but innovation.

He also knew this was unquestioningly the most public takeover he'd done. Everyone had an opinion or twelve, and no one—not a single person—was pleased.

But they would be. He would work hard to clean out the deadwood and make it a safe place for his software people to flourish with just the right amount of management.

He wanted to make this a place where people liked to come to work, where they were given a chance to create. And he needed it to be a place where his employees thought he was the epitome of success and professionalism. Because he was civilized. Smart. Not at all wolfy.

The intercom buzzed about ten minutes later. "Helene is here, sir."

"Send her in, please."

The door opened, and the sleek fox shifter who managed the app coding team walked in. He rose, then motioned her to a chair.

"Ah, Helene. Thank you for coming up." He studied her neat, stylish appearance and intelligent face.

"Yes, sir. How can I help?" She didn't seem the least bit worried.

He sat back down after she did. "So I just lost another manager."

"Oh? Let me guess. Gaines?" She rolled her eyes. "Gaines had an affair with Carl's sister-in-law. It was a mess."

"Ah. Well, yes, not to put too fine a point on it. So does Carl have something on everyone?"

"No. No, not me. Not most of us. He's just a...a...bad kitty." She shuddered. "And a mean one. He gathered all the like minds in the company to be his minions too."

"Is he likely to go after the Pallas cat and the little omega wolf?" He crossed his arms over his chest to hold in his growl at the thought, waiting to hear her opinion.

"Oh... I hadn't considered that. I'll have Adrian work from home, but I have no control over Isaac." She tapped her nails on the arm of the chair, clearly agitated.

"No, and he has to be here to work the mail room... I'll have someone keep an eye on both of them. That will just be easier for the time being, rather than having them shelter at home or take time off."

She looked vaguely confused. "So—do I call Adrian in? I'm not sure what you want me to do, exactly."

"I just wanted to get the lay of the land. If you think Carl might go after him, on the short term at least, I'll just have someone keep an eye on him. Let him come and go as usual. Working from home might make him more of a target. Someone could get to him easily in an apartment." He'd looked into where Adrian lived.

"Oh dear..." Helene frowned. "I don't like the idea of my people getting hurt."

"No. I don't either. Anyway, I also have to move someone up..."

"Oh, no. I don't want anything in sales." She made a

face that spoke of utter distaste. "But I can suggest a few good go-getters who are also decent beings."

She rose in Symon's estimation, just like that. "I'd love your recommendations. What are your employment goals?"

Helene smiled. "I love my programmers. Love them. They need reminders to eat and to nap and to, goddess help me, bathe."

"So you like managing the techies. Are you willing to take on more than one team?" He could really use someone like Helene as they expanded.

"I'll take on a lot, if you get me help. I don't want to do a half-assed job."

"I can do that." He wanted to fist pump the air, but he held back. "I reward good work, and I never ask more of people than they can give. And if I do, you have to tell me." He was fair that way. In fact, he was never as hard on anyone else as he was on himself.

Well, maybe his brothers.

"Okay. I'll go for it."

He held out a hand to shake again, just to seal the deal, and she grasped his hand firmly.

"So, tell me more about Adrian."

"He's a sweetheart. He is the center of the team in charge of speeding up the interface. He's done amazing work, and his team loves working with him. He works from home quite a bit—he tends to put in way more hours than he charges us for."

"He seems to be willing to stand up for what's right." In fact, watching Adrian throw himself in front of Isaac had made his stomach twist. Carl could really have hurt Adrian, and then Symon feared he would have ripped Carl's throat out.

That was the last thing on earth he needed to have happen.

He was here to prove that werewolves were suave, debonair. Controlled.

"He totally is. Even if it's not in his best interest." She gave him a wry smile. "But then Isaac is even more vulnerable than Adrian, so I can see why he did it. Adrian has a soft spot for those less toothy."

"Ah. Well, I can see that. So do I." And he had a soft spot for Adrian, apparently. More like a really hard one. "I appreciate him for it."

"I'm glad. He's a brilliant engineer. Such a sweetheart, so long as there's caffeine, pizza, and Insomnia cookies."

He raised an eyebrow. "What on earth are those?"

"Oh my god." She pulled out her phone to open up an app. "Look. You can order cookie delivery all night long. Well, all day too, but warm chocolate chip cookies in the middle of the night? A tech geek's dream."

"Oh...they have peanut butter ones."

"Right? The best." Helene hummed low in her throat.

"My, my." He would so order those and devour them on Stan's night off. Stan would never know, and if he did, well, so be it.

"Yeah. It's a thing."

"Well, thanks for that, and for the information."

"Anytime. Holler if you need me." She smiled and stood, hand held out to him.

"I will." He shook her hand one last time, then let her walk out, head held high, before he called his private security manager. Not the one for the building, but his personal guy.

"Hello?"

"Cy. I need your help on a project."

"Absolutely! Point me and shoot me."

"I have a Pallas cat and an omega wolf who need eyes on them. They both work at my new company, and they ran afoul of a puma shifter I just fired."

"Ooh…nummy goodness. Do I protect them or hunt the kitty?" Cy's joy was ridiculous.

"Well, maybe it would be better to keep an eye on the cat. The puma." Symon pondered that. "I can watch over the wolf since he works in my area of the office. But the Pallas is in the mail room…"

"I'll send little Bill down. Give him a job close to the Pallas cat. He needs practice."

"That sounds great. You hunt the big cat. Keep him off my guys. And I'll watch the wolf."

"Perfect. Send the deets. I'll send Bill your way. He's a good kid, eager to do a good job."

"I like that. You know it. Bill me."

"I will. How's Quin? I hear he got busted."

"You hear everything. Rian is working on it."

"Of course he is. He'll holler if he needs me." Cy's laughter seemed to fill the phone line.

"He will." Rian was so damn stubborn, but at least he kept his temper, unlike Quincy.

"Anyway, send me the stuff on your former employee and the protection-worthy kitty. I'll get on it. And if you want me to take the wolf—"

"No." He cleared his throat. "No I can do that."

"Cool. Enjoy."

Now why would Cy say that?

"Sure. How's it going otherwise?" He was so not going to ask what Cy meant.

"Good. Normal shit, you know? Just plain old, plain old."

"Yeah. I mean, no, I don't know lately. I've been doing a corporate takeover."

"You need a vacay soon, man."

"Mmm." Symon kept that noncommittal.

"Seriously. Go for a run under the moon. Dance a little. Skinny dip. I love skinny dipping."

"I don't do that, Cy." No, none of that qualified as controlled. In fact, it all sort of registered as reckless.

"You'd like it though. I know it. I'll find you a pretty omega to do it with..."

"Shut up." He had to grin at the idea. Somehow, when he thought about it, however briefly, it was Adrian he saw in his mind's eye.

"Shutting up, boss. One day, if you don't let the steam off, you'll explode."

"Yep. Kaboom. It'll be great. Just think how much money Quin and Rian will make selling the story." That was a terrible joke. His brothers would call up his soul and keep it in a bottle if he left them.

"They'd never let you go. None of us would."

"I know. That actually makes me feel better about myself." He blew out a breath. "Okay, I need to get back to work."

"Good deal. I've got your back, boss."

"I know you do. Talk to you soon. I'll send those files." He hung up, then sent Cy the files on all of the main players.

Except Adrian.

Adrian was his.

His body tightened, and he pushed it down, the need. That was ridiculous. Adrian just needed protection. That was all.

And if he wanted to fantasize a little in the deep of the night? Who would care?

CHAPTER

FOUR

Adrian hated when the code was twitchy, when he didn't know what was wrong, or why?

He hated it worse when he had to fix it at the office.

Helene had called all-hands-on-deck for the first week of the new boss's tenure, except now it was Friday night, and he had a bit of code to scrub.

Sucked to be the only guy in his department.

Maybe he should go down to troubleshooting and ask for company.

Someone would come up, he'd bet. Someone who wanted to share a pizza. Or some cookies.

He stood, stretching tall, his back popping. At the very least, he could go get a Coke.

He headed to the break room. The fridge was stocked with soda, energy drinks, protein shakes—all the things. It wasn't home, but it didn't suck.

Except that they didn't have his Dr Pepper, dammit.

That meant the vending machine.

He sighed, pulling his wallet out of his pocket. He really didn't want to walk down two floors. Or up one.

"Stupid. Just have a Coke."

But he didn't want a Coke. He wanted a Dr Pepper.

So he trudged up, because then down would be easier. Maybe no one would be up there to ask for help, but he wouldn't have to climb all the way back to his office.

He'd just reached the break room upstairs, his card at the ready to get a drink, when he heard an office door open. His scalp prickled. Who could be up here?

He found himself sniffing, his wolf refusing to stay still. Someone smelled rich, musky. Hot. His mouth watered a little, and he wanted to whine.

Except he wasn't that way. He was just a little city tech wolf. Not a beast of the woods.

"Who's there?" Footsteps came closer, and he knew that voice. Adrian almost groaned. The new boss.

"Just getting a Coke." No one but a little tech mouse from R&D. No one you want to bother. Shoo.

"Ah." The boss appeared in the doorway, and the smile that cut across his stern face surprised Adrian utterly. "Adrian. Hello. You're here late."

"I am. I have coding to fix." He didn't know exactly what to say, but he found himself grinning too. "I was in need of caffeine. You want one? I have more cash."

"No. No, thank you. In fact, I was coming out because I was about to go grab my supper at the security desk."

"Oh. Well, I won't keep you."

"Would you like to join me? I got enough pizza for three people, but everyone abandoned me."

"I—" His belly snarled at the thought of pizza.

He closed his eyes. So embarrassing.

"Come on. We'll take the elevator down. That way it will be nice and hot."

"Okay." What was he supposed to say? He was clearly starving. "Unless Willie eats it."

"The security guy? I ordered him a small deep dish. All the meats."

"Oh, you so rock!" He loved that, when people were kind.

"He works long and lonely hours. It's the least I can do." Symon ushered him into the elevator.

"That's really cool. Willie has been at this building for years." Willie was a bear, and he wasn't particularly into company, but he was warm and protective.

"So I've heard from Helene."

"Oh, is she your informant?"

"She is. She's a font of useful information." Symon's warm hand landed on his lower back, making him jump. It sort of made his tail want to wag.

"She's a good manager." But hopefully she was being quiet about them.

"She is. And she loves all of you guys."

Well, that sounded good, didn't it?

"I'm glad. She's cool." Cool. He was such a dipshit.

"I like her." They headed into the lobby when the bell dinged, and that was enough pizza for everyone left in the building, not just three people... "Ah, Willie. Did you get your pizza?"

"Yes, sir. Thank you."

"Can you call the guys in troubleshooting and tell them the pizza is on me?" Symon grabbed two pizza boxes. "Adrian and I will be in the development area if anyone wants to bring another pizza up and join us."

"You got it. Thank you." Willie bowed his big head in thanks.

"You are very welcome."

"I could just take the pizzas down to troubleshooting for you."

"Oh I would much rather have your company."

What was he supposed to say to that?

"Well, the break room has a table. It's comfy." That was good, right? He was saying the right thing?

He wanted to, because the scent of the boss was heady, making him shudder.

"That's great." Symon gave him another glinting grin. Wow. He really was so attractive.

"You're working late for a Friday..." Go small talk.

"I'm not going to expect the team to do anything I won't. When Helene called, I came back in."

"Oh, I'm fixing it. Don't worry. I'll be able to work it out."

"I believe you. I'm just here for support, and I always have work to do. Plus Helene wanted me to see how things happened."

"Ah. Well, that makes sense."

Adrian worried that Helene was going to become upper management, like one of the executives. He'd hate to lose her.

"I'm pleased. I want to know the company inside and out. I offered her a promotion, you know."

"Huh?" He wasn't sure he was following.

"Helene. She said she'd take on more of the team as a den mother, and she'd take a raise, but not a promotion. She loves you guys."

"Oh..." He almost teared up. "She's good to us. Seriously."

"I can tell. I'm glad you know it, though." They arrived at the break room, and they had it to themselves. They sat across from each other, and his mouth watered.

"Let's eat. You're starving."

"I ate last night. I just was getting a Coke." He took a piece as soon as the boss did.

"Last night? That's twenty-four hours ago." Symon stared at him. "That's not good for you, Adrian."

He did a lot of things that weren't good for him. "I had coffee. I like coffee and cream."

"Hmmm." That frown was a little worrisome, but Symon just opened a pizza box and gave him a cheesy, melty piece.

Oh. God.

It was hot and had just the right amount of spice and meat. He loved it. "Where did you order this?" he asked around a mouthful. "I've never had it before."

"Willie suggested it. Paisano's?"

"Huh." He shrugged. They ordered from the menus in the break room. "Well, it's yum."

He would swear Symon's eyes flashed a bright gold for a moment. "It certainly is."

Except he hadn't had a bite yet, had he?

Maybe he'd missed it.

He ate, his nose searching for Symon's scent.

He found it, hotter and spicier than the pizza, and it made him moan. Under his breath, he hoped.

Symon leaned forward, napkin in hand, to wipe his cheek. "A little cheese."

"Oh. Oh, sorry." He caught himself turning to nuzzle the touch. What was wrong with him?

He didn't do this!

He never did this.

Symon watched him, gaze never leaving his. "No, don't apologize." Those rough fingers stroked his cheek. Where did a CEO get calluses like that?

"I—" His wolf wanted to wiggle and bark, show his belly. "Is your pizza okay?"

"It's perfect." Symon drew back to take a bite. "Salty and spicy."

"Yes." Was Symon salty and spicy? Oh, no. No thinking that. "Those are my favorite flavors. I mean, I like sweet, too."

"So do I." Symon took another bite, those white teeth tearing at the cheese. It made him flush to watch it, made him feel kind of pervy.

You have to be good, man. You're a loner. You aren't a part of a pack. At all.

He licked his lips. Cleared his throat. "So are they all the same? The pizzas?" Because his piece was gone.

"No, there are others. The one here is chicken and jalapeno and feta."

"Yeah? That sounds yummy, really. Do you want some?" He wanted to watch the boss eat it. He could fantasize about it for weeks.

"Yes. I do." Symon opened the box and pulled them both out a piece. He bit into it, pulling the cheese long, then lapping it up, and Adrian went instantly hard.

He whimpered, licking his lips like he could taste the big wolf right here.

"Eat up," Symon told him, watching him like the big hunter he was. He was so effortlessly alpha. So damn commanding. And Adrian wanted him. It was like a porn movie, only prettier.

He hated that about himself. He wanted to ride the huge male like a prized pony.

It was ridiculous and perfect and absolutely delicious.

"This is really good. Spicy." He covered his confusion with eating.

"Mmmhmm." Symon leaned toward him across the table. "Very much so."

Was he panting? He thought he was panting. His entire body wanted to wag. He held himself very still, trying not to give what he was feeling away, but he probably stank of need.

In fact, Symon's nostrils were twitching. It was no fair.

He choked as he tried to breathe instead of swallow. Whoops.

"Oh, are you okay?" Symon hopped up to come clap him on the back.

He hacked and wheezed, his eyes rolling back at his own stupidity. Classy. Sexy. Go him.

Finally his body let air in, and he whooped for it, breathing deep.

"I got you." Symon opened his Coke. "Have a sip."

He drank deep, sucking the drink down. "Please. I'm sorry."

"No worries. None at all." Symon rubbed between his shoulder blades gently.

He was so damn embarrassed. God. But that hand felt really good on him, and he wanted to lean into it again. He was such a sucker.

He needed to remember who he was, what he wanted, and what he didn't.

Symon finally sat back down, then grabbed a slice. "So what went wrong?"

"Went wrong? With the code?" He was so lost.

"Yes. Helene really couldn't explain it to me, but I want to try to understand everything." Symon munched, watching him carefully. There was a shrewdness to those eyes. A sharp intelligence.

"There was a bit that seems to have corrupted. Weird, because we just ran it, but it happens. Once I found it, it's an easy fix. I'm running a test. It shouldn't take long."

Symon's gaze sharpened even more. "Could someone have sabotaged it?"

"What?" His eyebrows went up. "Who? Why?"

"Well, I've fired a couple of high-level guys. Do they have loyal people who would do that out of spite?"

His eyes went wide, a low growl escaping him. "They wouldn't."

"I don't know. I mean, I know things corrupt in code all the time. But didn't your team just roll out a new version that was tested within an inch of its life?" Symon waited, chewing a bite.

"We did. It took me all day to find the little bugger. All day." Dammit.

"Yeah. I worry, especially about the cat. He had long arms here."

"Carl? Yeah. He was a dick, and he was like...sneaky."

"Yes. And he had at least three people quit when I fired him. I just worry someone is still hanging around who decided to fight from within."

"Well, I'll go look at the keystrokes." He'd dig himself up some information and make this shit work.

"That sounds good. I'll come with you." Symon boxed the pizza back up.

"You're sure more hands-on than our last CEO was toward the end of his reign."

"You have no idea."

Something about that dark, rich tone in Symon's voice made him flush deeply and swallow hard.

Work.

Work first.

Then...escape.

Otherwise he was just going to embarrass himself. He always did around alphas. And he'd never met one like this before. No one had ever revved his engine like Symon. Ever.

All he had to do was figure out what had happened, and then...

Well, then, he guessed he would tell Symon who it was.

CHAPTER

FIVE

Symon had watched Adrian work a good bit of the night. In fact, the guy had never let up except to grab a piece of cold pizza and munch on it.

And he'd fixed the app, but he was still trying to find out how the code had broken.

And it was almost dawn.

"Adrian, you need to get some rest."

"No. Go on home. I'm so close."

"I don't think so. Someone made sure to hide their tracks. You need to come back with fresh eyes." He couldn't bear to watch Adrian drink another Coke.

"I—I have to." Those pretty eyes were bright red. He needed to call them a car. There was room at his place.

"No." He dialed his driver. "I need a pickup at the office." He drove himself a lot, but he'd had Rudy drive him in when the emergency call came in, knowing he might be too tired by the time he went home. And he liked to have a driver so he could work in the car.

"Yes, sir. On my way."

"I'll take you home, or you can come back to my house, but you're done working today."

Those big eyes blinked up at him, so exhausted.

"Your house?"

"Yes. It's safer for you there."

"Safer?" Adrian blinked harder. "Why wouldn't I be safe at home?"

"Because if someone is willing to sabotage the code, they might be up for going after the only guy who can fix it."

"Oh, I doubt that..."

He didn't. In fact, he didn't doubt it a bit. Symon's instincts insisted that he needed to protect this omega.

"I'm rarely wrong about the big picture." Symon put a hand on Adrian's shoulder. "Come on. And bring your laptop."

"Let me log out of the big computer too. That way they can't use my passwords."

"Good man." Well, at least Adrian was going to stop arguing.

Adrian shut his console down, and started packing up. He smelled of sugar and worry, and Symon wanted to scoop him up and hold him.

"Come on, honey. My driver is picking us up." He scented the air as he opened the door of the workroom, then steered Adrian to the elevator.

"All right. I'll just go to the apartment. Catch some z's and then finish it in a bit."

"No. I want you to come with me. I'll bring you back in tomorrow." Symon offered Adrian the least wolfish smile he had. "I have a big house. You'll be safe and comfortable."

"I—Is that weird?"

"Not at all. I want you to be in a safe place." And if he

just took Adrian back to his apartment, he would end up working again in an hour. If they went to his house, Adrian would be an hour out of town and without a ride.

"Oh. Okay."

"Night, Willie," he said as they passed the security desk. "Be on the lookout for Carl or his people."

"Yessir." Willie nodded. "That's a bad one. I've heard things."

"Well, I'll be careful. Believe me. I have a strong pack."

"Good deal." Willie waved them out, and he walked Adrian outside, where they stood in the chilly early-morning air, waiting.

Adrian shivered, the poor little wolf so exhausted, so worn through.

The car pulled up, and he handed Adrian in, then slid in next to him, and he stilled Adrian with a touch of his hand, keeping him from sliding away to the other end of the seat.

"Thanks, Rudy. Just in time. It was getting cold."

"No worries, sir. Sit back and relax and I'll take you home."

He leaned back in the seat, grateful for the seat warmers, even through his suit jacket. When Adrian shivered again, Symon pulled him close, sharing body heat.

"S-s-sorry. I have a chill."

"You're exhausted. It's understandable."

"I didn't think I was that bad. I guess..." A light snore sounded, Adrian dropping right off.

He rumbled softly, keeping the sweet body close. Poor sweet omega. He wanted Adrian badly, but he wasn't going to push. This one needed rest.

Care.

Attention.

It was almost undeniable.

He wanted more of Adrian altogether.

"Tough day, boss?" Rudy asked quietly.

"Just a long one. He worked hard."

"Looks like it. Hate it when the omegas are over-worked." Rudy was a very traditional alpha, and his omega was treated like a pasha.

"Yes. And someone did this deliberately, I'm sure of it." He was going to find out who, too.

"Well, he'll be safe as houses at yours. We'll make sure of it." That little growl was certain.

"Yes. I'll be on top of it, Rudy. He's a good man." He could tell how much Adrian cared about things.

And there was something about the wolf resting against his arm. It was impossible not to adore him. He was just totally unassuming, utterly geeky. So amazing. And he smelled good. Right.

His brothers were going to give him no end of shit, for buying a company to find an omega.

He grinned, leaning his head back and closing his eyes. That didn't really matter, did it? His brothers gave him crap about everything...

He spread his arm out over the top of the seat, and Adrian almost immediately crawled into his lap, snuggling close. Someone was craving affection. And he was going to give it.

Rudy gave him a smile in the rearview, and he nodded. Yes. This one was his.

His mate.

His breath caught in his chest. Fuck him.

This was his mate.

He shook his head, the denial instinctive, but Symon knew it was true. He wasn't one for wolfy instinct, but dammit, that was exactly what he was feeling.

What the fuck was he going to do?

He blew out a long breath, forcing himself to relax. To focus.

He was going to start this morning by wooing Adrian with breakfast. Clearly he didn't eat right.

Obviously the omega needed care and feeding, and he could get Stan to make bacon. Bacon cured all manner of ills.

And then he would set about cementing the mate bond.

First, sleep, food, a bath, some soft amazing clothes.

Then more food, some wine, a nap, more food.

He dozed, and Rudy hit a soft chime when they were almost home instead of talking, which woke him and let him gently ease Adrian away from him to pull him out of sleep as well. "We're here."

"Oh. Oh, I fell asleep. I'm sorry."

"No worries." *You were warm and heavy in my lap. I loved it.*

"How embarrassing." Adrian rubbed his eyes, then peered out the window. "Where are we?"

"At my house. I'm in the mountains. Come on. We can have some breakfast after we take a shower."

"Together?" Adrian's voice cracked.

Symon smiled. "Well, if you like."

"It's probably not good for my career..."

"How could it be bad? I'm not the type to worry about it."

"Hmm."

Symon stepped out of the car. "Come on, sweet. Rudy, thank you. Go be with your Harley."

"Thanks, boss. Y'all have a great weekend." He saluted and pulled away.

Adrian watched him go, his expression very close to panic.

"Come on, sweet. We're not alone here. Stan, my house-keeper and personal assistant, is in there. He'll make bacon."

"Oh, cool. Because you make me hard, and it would be easy to be stupid. Like bend-over-and-beg-for-it stupid." Adrian clapped a hand over his mouth, eyes wide.

"I'm not going to complain about that, Adrian. You make me hard as well."

"We—Bacon? I love bacon?" *Are there eggs too?*

There are. And toast. Or biscuits. Do you like biscuits? He took Adrian's arm to steer him inside.

Adrian's head tilted. "I love biscuits. With strawberry jam... Did you?"

"Did I what?" Butter wouldn't melt in his mouth, but he didn't want Adrian to freak out. "Strawberry jam is the best, though Stan also does an empowering apricot."

"I've never had that, but honey butter is amazing..."

"Oh. Yum. Yes. I know Stan has that in the fridge. I like it on the fry bread he makes."

"Wow. I mean, how do you ever leave the house if you have someone who cooks like that?"

"Ah, well, Stan does get time off."

"Do you cook?" *I burn water. I eat pizza and toaster pastries and tons of Insomnia cookies.*

I heard about these cookies. We'll have to see if we can get some the next time we're at the office together. Though he would put Stan's oatmeal scotchies up against anything.

They totally deliver there. You're a little far out, but you could get extras.

"Mmmm."

"Symon. You're all right?" Stan met them near the front door as they walked inside, tying the sash on his robe.

"I am. I would have texted, but I wanted to let you sleep as long as possible. This is Adrian. He'll be staying for a bit."

"Hey, there. You look exhausted. Are you both hungry?"

"Starving. We were thinking biscuits and bacon and such?"

"You got it. And... I'm thinking a nice herbal tea?"

Oh, excellent thought. "Thank you, Stan. There's been a lot of caffeine tonight."

"All-nighters tend to. This will ease the raging wolf."

"Mmmm. Thank you. Come on, Adrian. I'll show you where you can have a shower, and I can find you some clean clothes."

"Thank you? I—this is really weird..." But Adrian followed, blinking nice and slow.

"Hey, you're exhausted." He led Adrian to the guest bath. "Use the shower seat in case you fall asleep."

"You have a shower seat? Cool." Adrian shuffled into the bathroom, blinking owlishly.

"I do." He got the water going, adjusting the rain bath heads to Adrian's height sitting down. Then he pulled out fluffy towels and put them in the warmer. "Here, sweet. Let me help you."

"My head is pounding."

He understood that. His own was beginning to throb.

"You need a big glass of water. Get in the shower, hmm?" He helped Adrian strip down, then guided him into the shower and shut the door. "Be right back." Symon wanted to join Adrian badly, but he knew better. They both needed rest.

And he wanted to know Adrian was with him, all the way. No question. Wide-awake and wanting.

He could wait.

Symon got two bottles of water, then some soft sweats that Stan had laid out for him along with some fuzzy socks. He took them back to the bathroom so he could check on Adrian.

Adrian was resting on the seat, slowly washing his hair, the lean body stretched up tall.

He perched on the closed toilet, just waiting, jonesing on the sound of water hitting Adrian's skin. So damn fine.

He could scent the richness of Adrian's body, and he fought the urge to whimper. He was in control, dammit. Except when he tried yoga breathing, it brought more of Adrian's scent, and his cock rose up hard and proud.

"I can smell you. It's making me dizzy," Adrian admitted.

"I'm not sorry." That popped out. And it was true. "I can smell you too, and I want you." The words were a guttural growl in his throat.

"Why? Is it going to get me in trouble? I don't want to be in trouble."

"No. Not at all. But I'm trying to be hands-off until you're not work drunk and caffeine high."

"Mmm...that's sweet of you." Adrian turned under the spray, rinsing off, showing off a long, slender, hard cock.

So hot. And that tight little ass on the bench made him want to touch it. So he turned away. He felt stalkerish, mate or no. Adrian deserved to know what was happening, to come to it naturally.

When the water shut off, he turned to help.

"I love this shower. I've never seen one without a door."

"It's amazing, huh?" He chuckled. "Mine is even better. This is the guest shower."

"Better than this?" Adrian turned to give him a disbelieving stare.

"It's a whole room, essentially." He indulged himself in his private space.

"Oh. Wow. That's really—wow." *I have a frosted glass box.*

Well, you have an apartment...

Adrian tilted his head. *I— How do you do that?*

You'll find out.

I will. Adrian frowned deeply. *And I have a decent apartment, by the way.*

I'm sure you do. But they tend to come in one-size-fits-all with furnishings.

Adrian relaxed, laughing. "True. And I'm not allowed to upgrade."

"No, and why would you invest the money in something that isn't yours?"

"I guess. I mean, it would be nice to have a few luxuries."

"Well, you can enjoy mine." He handed Adrian the towel, reluctant to lose the idea of him bare, but the water was off.

"Thanks." Adrian wrapped himself up, almost getting lost in the terrycloth. He chuckled, standing so he could reach out to help.

"I brought you some of Stan's clean sweats. He's far more of a size with you than I am."

"Thank you. I'm way more awake now." Adrian dressed quickly, drying his hair with the towel.

"Better?"

"Much."

"Hungry?"

"I thought there was no way I could be after all that pizza, but I'm starving."

"Me too." Symon held out a hand, relieved when Adrian dropped his towel in the hamper and grabbed Symon, meshing their fingers. "Don't worry. It's all going to be okay. We just need food and rest, right?"

"Yeah. Then we'll be able to think."

"Mmm. Or something." He had a feeling that no matter what he did, Adrian would be a distraction.

In fact, Symon was willing to bet on it.

"Late dinner or early breakfast is ready!" Stan called.

"Come on, sweet. Let's get some food and then we can nap." He was feeling dozy from the heat of the shower and, now that Adrian was dressed, well, he was less involved in porny thoughts.

"That sounds like heaven." Adrian squeezed his fingers. "I feel like I'm in some weird sort of dream, you know?"

"I do know. I feel it too." He brought Adrian's hand up to his mouth to kiss, feeling the electric shock that passed from him to Adrian and back.

Adrian sucked in a harsh breath, and that pointed chin lifted. The urge to nibble the pale column of throat was enough to make Symon's eyes cross.

"Breakfast," Adrian said. "Juice. Stuff like that."

"I could nibble you."

"Breakfast!" Stan called again. Louder.

Symon sighed. "Harshing my fun. Stan is all about self-denial."

"Is he? That seems...sad. Is he okay?"

"He is sad. But I think he's getting better all the time. He's had a rough time of things in his life." And the rest wasn't his story to tell. "I probably shouldn't talk out of turn. He's an incredibly kind, good man. A natural caregiver."

Adrian patted his arm. "Of course. I wasn't being ugly. I just hate when people aren't happy. It happens a lot. Like a lot, a lot."

"Yeah?" *Are you an empath, honey? Is that why you work alone?*

Adrian blinked up at him, eyes suddenly huge, glowing a bright silver like the moon at its fullest.

Lord help him. Adrian was just shining with magic.

Easy, little one. I have you.

I'm okay. The magic was barely contained, and, when Adrian stumbled toward him, Symon caught him instinctively, and there was no denying the sudden spark that bound them.

He pulled Adrian up against his chest to kiss him, because he had to. There was no choice.

Adrian almost crawled up his body, a wildfire building in his spine.

He grabbed that tight little ass, lifting Adrian to him, and they both panted for air for a moment before they dove back into the kiss.

He stumbled to the kitchen counter, tongue fucking Adrian's sweet mouth. Stan had disappeared, which was probably good. This wasn't supposed to be a show.

Adrian's legs wrapped around his waist, hips moving in a steady, undeniable rhythm. They rubbed together, and Symon growled, because the need to claim Adrian rode him hard.

"Do it." Adrian shoved at his clothes. "Please. I want you."

"Are you sure? I want you to be sure, Adrian. No regrets later."

Adrian growled back at him. "I'm not a virgin. I've been fucked before."

"This isn't about just fucking." Adrian had to see that. "This is way more than something so simple."

"I meant that you won't hurt me. Unless you leave me aching like that."

"I won't hurt you. Not unless it's in a fun way and we both agree to it." He bared his teeth, then pulled off Adrian's sweats.

"Funny. I'm aching, man. All the way to the bone. I'm wet for you."

"I can smell you, sweet. You make my mouth water. I want inside you." He tore off his own clothes.

"Now." Adrian stripped down, right there in the kitchen.

"Yes, now." He lifted Adrian again, spreading him wide and pinning him against the counter.

Stan might kill him, but he'd worry about that later. At the moment, he only had the energy and attention for Adrian, who was molten hot and wet against his hand as Symon checked his readiness.

"Fuck... I'm ready. I mean it. I'm so ready for you." That slick hole fluttered against his fingers, and it made him want to howl.

"God, baby." Adrian wasn't sweet just this second, so that moniker didn't work. Here he was heated and wiggling and begging. Naughty puppy.

And Adrian was going to be *his* naughty puppy, dammit. He wasn't sure how or why, and he didn't really care right now, but he knew it, down in his bones.

He bent to bite at Adrian's collarbone, his cock sliding along that wet hole, the tip slipping right in. It took his breath. Adrian was made for him.

"More." Adrian's heels dug into his hips.

"Anything you want." He thrust up, desperate to be sunk deep into Adrian. He wanted to rut.

As if Adrian heard him, his pup slammed down, taking him down to the root.

"Fuck!" He all but howled the words, and he had to go completely still while he fought for control of his body. He'd promised not to hurt Adrian, and if he moved just right, he undoubtedly would. He was too caught up in what was happening. It was too fucking primal.

Symon grabbed those lean hips. "Don't you even breathe, baby. Just give me a minute. I need it."

"One minute. I need your knot. I want to feel you all inside me, and I want it now."

"I can tell, baby. You're so wet. So hot. I'm going to give you all you need. I just need to fucking breathe." He was in control here, not Adrian. He called the damn shots. And he wanted to savor this, even if it did go fast once it got moving.

He needed to make sure that Adrian soared, that he spun with pleasure and came over and over.

Adrian squirmed. "I need more. Please. I'm burning up. I need your knot. I need you to come."

"And you need too, huh?" He palmed Adrian's cock. Symon was where he needed to be now. He could hold on. Even if sweat was pouring off his skin. God, he was hot as hell.

And Adrian made him nuts. No one had ever gotten to him like this.

"Uh-huh. Come on. Please. I can feel how much you need. It's so fucking hot. I can feel everything."

"I've got you, Adrian. Right here. I'm going to fuck you until you scream. I'm going to make you see stars."

"Promises, promises." Adrian chuckled breathlessly. "You feel so good."

"So do you, baby." He flexed his hips, pressing up and forward. He moved slowly, dragging it out to begin with, but he knew it was going to be a wild ride.

Adrian's smile was wondering, tickled, and his pup surged up, slamming their mouths together.

He groaned, his body on fire, his muscles straining. His lungs heaved like bellows. Damn. It was so fine.

He punched up with his hips, bracing his legs so he could move faster and harder. His control was slipping again, but he couldn't care.

More. More. I have waited for so long! The thought was piercing, driven into his brain.

Oh, damn, baby. He went into overdrive, sawing back and forth. His knot rose, filling Adrian more. Pushing both their limits.

Adrian took him, body perfect and heated around him. Those muscles squeezed down on his cock, and he grunted, his damn eyes crossing.

He was losing his mind, and he knew it. It was absolutely maddening.

Somehow that didn't matter a bit. He had to go with it. And it felt so damn perfect. He could barely breathe for how good it felt, and his muscles felt as if they were seizing up.

Adrian clenched around him, and he gasped, energy shooting through him. He pressed as deep as he could, grinding with his hips.

"Oh, please. I feel your knot. It's almost there."

"Almost?" If he got any more swollen he might explode and go like a rocket. His ass clenched, and he slammed inside Adrian, and finally that got him the wail of happiness he wanted to hear.

"Yes! There. Right there. Symon! Alpha! Oh my god."

He growled, pleased to finally have made Adrian call his name. "That's it, baby. Give me more of that."

Adrian howled, the sounds of his mate's need coloring the room and making him want to bite the air.

He snapped at Adrian's shoulder again, just grazing with his canine teeth, and Adrian almost screamed, going rigid against him. He felt the drops of precome against his belly as Adrian shook, not quite able to come yet.

He held them right there, hands bracketing Adrian's hips to actually keep him still for a moment. And that got him a whine of frustration.

The glow in Adrian's eyes was the single hottest thing he'd ever seen, and he luxuriated in it.

He pumped into Adrian, so close to filling him with seed that it was hard to hold back. So he reached down between them to stroke Adrian's cock, needing him to come. They were fully engaged by the knot now. He wasn't moving.

Not in any real way. They needed to finish this so they could do it again with breakfast in bed.

"Please, Symon. Take me over the edge. Please."

Sweet wolf.

"Now, Adrian. Come for me now." He bucked, and he squeezed with his hand, and that was it.

Adrian shouted, his head falling back, cords standing out in his neck as he shot.

That pulled Symon over too, and he yelled, his nuts pulling up, his knot feeling like a balloon bursting. Jesus. He might not survive this.

Adrian panted, his little wolf limp and heavy against the counter. "Whoa."

"Mmm." He held them up, his head leaning on Adrian's,

their mingled scent heavy in his nose. Nothing had ever smelled better.

Not even breakfast, which was a pretty nice odor in its own right. He had no idea what day it was. French toast wasn't a regular for Stan.

He had to figure out how to carry Adrian with one arm and all the breakfast with the other, with his pants around his knees and his knot in Adrian.

So he managed to step out of his pants, and he headed for the bedroom. Adrian never stirred, which was good, because there was a slight throat clearing.

"I'll bring a breakfast tray, Symon."

"Thank you, Stan. It smells so good. And I'm starving."

A soft chuckle was his only answer, and he carried Adrian to the bedroom.

They needed to talk, but they had time. Now was for lazy sleep and food and cuddling his new mate.

Bonding.

And he was starting immediately.

CHAPTER

SIX

Adrian woke up and he had no idea where he was for a long moment.

He was alone in a bed big enough for four of him stacked both directions. The smell of something comforting and amazing wafted across his senses, and he sniffed.

Potato soup? He hoped so. He loved potato soup.

He blinked at the long shadows on the floor. How long had he slept? He'd gone to bed early in the morning. With Symon. And breakfast.

Oh, goddess. His cheeks heated until he was sure they were going to flame out and boil his brain. He'd had sex with Symon. In the kitchen. He'd begged for it. He'd gotten himself knotted.

He was supposed to be on heat suppressants.

How had that happened?

The thing was, after the initial panic, his mind stopped rabbiting and his body relaxed. Symon had given him what he'd needed. What he'd asked for. But he'd tried not to.

He'd told Adrian to be very sure. Symon wouldn't ever hurt him. Somehow he just knew it.

Which, okay, didn't make him shouting, "Knot me now," less embarrassing, but he wasn't in any danger or anything.

Now, where was the en suite? He didn't want to run to the guest bath naked.

How hard could it be? One door would be a hall, one or two would be a closet, and one would be the en suite, right?

Right.

He found the window, and headed to the left. It had to be the bathroom.

Sure enough, it was a super luxurious bathroom, and he did his business, then looked around before ducking into the shower. He'd been in bed with Symon a long time, and he was a little crusty.

Maybe more than a little.

"Adrian? Are you all right?"

Oh, fuck. Now he was nude in the man's shower without asking.

"I—Yes?" He was naked and wet in someone else's house.

"Okay. Can I come in?"

His body heated. "Yes." That was way better than thinking.

"Good answer." Symon slid into the shower, fingers wrapping around his hips. "You get some sleep?"

"Did you?"

"Yes. I had to make a few calls, and I wanted to tell Stan what to make for supper."

"Is it potato soup? It smells like potato soup."

"Mmm. Isaac told me the other day how much you liked it."

"What? He did? When?"

"When I called him to see if I could send him some soup. He likes chicken and wild rice."

"I know! I'm just surprised he opened up that much."

"He's a nice guy," Symon said, sounding amused. "And much more the kind of person I like to talk to than the suits."

"He's great. We're buddies, you know? We play a lot of FPSs online."

Symon blinked at him. "That's video games, right?"

"Yes."

"Ah. I play Mario Kart."

"Yeah? Me too! It makes me laugh so hard." He loved all the goofy little guys.

"I love the weird dune buggy car." Symon reached for him, and he was quickly becoming addicted to showers with this man. Wet. Soapy. Hot as hell. All hard...

"We should play. Can I play with the boss?" His fingers found Symon's cock and circled it.

"Uh-huh. You can totally play, baby." Symon watched him, gold glints flashing in his eyes.

He hadn't expected an alpha to play, not like this. He tightened his fingers, stroking Symon from base to tip.

Symon bared his teeth, but his eyes danced with humor. "That's perfect, baby."

"Mmhmm..." Symon's cock was absolutely perfect, fat and thick and long. He double-fisted it, pulling hand over hand.

Rocking into his touch, Symon grunted, eyes closing. "Don't stop, now. You feel so goddamn good."

"Not going to it." Except he might, because he wanted to kneel down and suck.

Did that make him slutty? He thought maybe it did...

But when they were this close to each other, he didn't care. Later he might. But not now.

He didn't even have to kneel. There was a shower seat that put him in the right height.

Yummy.

He took that heavy cock between his lips, sucking it in deep, and drawing it into the back of his throat.

"Uhn. Baby." Symon sank a hand into his hair, massaging, and fuck, it felt so good.

He arched into the touch, begging for more. It made him tingle all the way to his toes—that touch made him moan.

That heavy cock tasted perfect on his tongue, the column of flesh throbbing. Symon was just fucking right, and he loved it.

He couldn't get enough.

"That's it, baby. You can take all you want." Symon petted him, his cheeks and neck and shoulders, and he grabbed that tight ass and held on tight.

He sucked, swaying back and forth with the force of his motions. And the salty drops he got for his trouble were pure addiction.

He swallowed, taking them in, and learning the flavor of—his alpha—the boss.

"Mmmm. Come on, baby. Bring it home. Then I'll play with you."

Play with him.

He groaned, head bobbing as he swallowed, his hands rolling Symon's heavy balls.

"Fuck!" Symon went up on his toes, and that cock seemed to fucking dance in his mouth as Symon came.

Oh, that was lovely and quick, proving how much the alpha wanted him.

"Get up here." The jets of come in his mouth had barely stopped when Symon yanked him to his feet.

He dangled for a second, and it felt embarrassingly hot, to need so much. Then Symon wrapped an arm around him, hugging him close with one hand while reaching down to stroke him with the other.

"Oh. Oh, fuck. Alpha." His eyes crossed, and he gasped.

"Does that feel so good, baby? I like how you like it." Symon tugged him hard and fast, giving him the best friction.

Did it? He thought it did. In fact, it felt frigging amazing, and he didn't want it to stop. So he humped like a naughty puppy and let Symon touch him until he wanted to scream with it, his whole body on fire.

"Please..." He wanted more. He wanted to come. He wanted Symon.

"I have you. I won't stop until you come, baby. I want you to show me how you feel." Symon's thumb swiped the head of his cock.

"Uh-huh." He arched back, his lips parting as he shot, his entire body convulsing.

"So hot, baby. That's perfect." Symon held him effortlessly.

"You made me crazy." His entire body was tingling.

"Good. Because you do the same for me." Symon kissed him. Hard.

Whoa. It was... That was... His eyes crossed. He wrapped his arms around Symon's neck, and Symon lifted him to carry him back into the bedroom.

"You hungry? I have sandwiches and chips..."

His belly answered with a desperate little growl.

"Let's do that then." Symon chuckled. "I think we worked up an appetite."

"I just—don't you want me to fix the coding?"

"You set everything up. Helene is dealing with it."

"Can you do that? It was my fix?" He didn't let people steal his coding.

"It's yours. Helene is fierce. And I won't have it any other way."

"She is. I'm glad you like her." Not *like* her like her, but her work.

"I do like her. And I adore you already. All of your parts, including your brilliant brain."

His cheeks began to burn, and he felt his entire body try to tighten.

"Come on, sweet. Eat first. Then more crazy sex."

He chuckled. "I know, right? It's nuts."

"It is, but we'll figure it out. Later. Not today. I need to explore this with you."

"Okay. That sounds good." Because he couldn't be in heat, right? So it was just the newness.

That sounded way more reasonable.

New relationship energy for the win.

CHAPTER
SEVEN

Symon didn't want to go back to work.

But by day three, the calls from Helene and his assistant were getting ever more frantic. They needed him and Adrian to come in, and they needed them now.

There had been another attack on the code.

Adrian was ready, his clothes cleaned and dried. "We need to go, boss. I need to access the servers from the source."

"I know. And I need to get my brother here." He needed to call Rian and get the family lawyer in on everything.

"What does he do?"

Walk around in expensive suits and make deals. He grinned. "He's a lawyer. He'll know who to apply pressure to."

"Oh. I don't know any lawyers." Of course Adrian didn't.

"Well, Rian is a damn good one." He grinned at Adrian. "Just let me tell Stan. I'll drive."

"Oh, you drive yourself sometimes?" Adrian teased.

Little shit.

"I even drive other people. Come on, baby. Let's hit it." He would just text Stan. They needed to get going.

"I'm ready when you are, boss." Adrian winked at him. "Lead the way."

They headed out to the garage, and he took the big black SUV instead of his sports car. It was less noticeable.

Adrian cuddled in with a hum. "Oh, this is a great car. I approve."

Little hedonist.

"It has heated seats." He liked the idea of warming Adrian's ass.

In fact, it gave him a happy.

"Yeah? Too cool. I love it."

"It gets the job done. Now. My other car takes the curves way better..."

"Yeah? What kind of car is it? I don't have one. I live close enough to walk."

That was wild, to not have a car in Denver. It wasn't a walking town.

"It's a Jag. I love it. Silly thing."

"No, that's cool. I just don't do anything but home and work."

"I'm on the road a lot. I want decent rides." And he had an embarrassing number of cars...

"That's neat. Where do you go? I mean, do you travel or do you mean Boulder to Denver? Do you ever go up in the mountains?"

"Yes. I like to hike and camp both. What about you?" Adrian didn't seem outdoorsy, but who knew?

"I haven't had the opportunity in a while. Little lone omegas in the woods equals stupidity, and I'm not dumb."

"Ah. Well, we should go together." No one would bother

Adrian with him, even if he wasn't the tooth-and-claw type.

And he could be to defend Adrian.

"Yeah? You want to?" Oh, that was eager.

"I do. Let's get this crisis dealt with and we'll find a cabin with a hot tub."

"Fair enough. Do you think anyone will notice I have the same clothes on as Friday?"

"Well, if they do, I doubt they'll say anything." At least Stan had washed and pressed said clothes. "And they're clean."

"They are, and that one seam was fixed too. So sweet."

"So if anything, people will think you did laundry." He reached over to squeeze Adrian's leg.

"No one would think that." Adrian's giggle was sweet as hell, erotic.

"No? Are you sure?"

"Nope. I'm a sniff-my-shirt-and-put-it-back-on guy. The fact that my clothes are so clean and pressed will be a sure walk of shame giveaway."

"Ah." He winked over. "We'll say it was for your protection."

"Oh, I like it. Witness Protection Alpha." That made Adrian applaud like crazy.

"Thank you." He bowed a tiny bit from the waist. "I did check in on Isaac, and he's fine, so it looks like whoever this is has decided the company is a better target than an individual."

"Oh, that's good."

His phone rang, his head of security's name popping up. Shit. Maybe he'd spoken too soon.

"Hello?"

"Sir, are you heading into the office?"

"I am. I got the call that there had been a cyberattack."

"Yes, well, I suggest you turn around. They've evacuated the building due to fire."

"A fire? In the building?" He started looking for the next exit to pull off. "What's the status?"

"No. In the building next door. 3299 Coal."

Adrian frowned. "Wait. What did he say? Where?"

"3299 Coal."

"That's my building! That's my building, Symon."

"One of the employees I was worried about for retaliation lives in that building. We need eyes on the situation."

"Of course, sir, but the firefighters have the block quarantined. I'll call you back. There's no way to get here right this second."

"I need to get home and check!" The scent of fear poured off his omega.

"They have the whole block quarantined. Call me back when you know something."

"Yes, sir."

Adrian sat there, eyes huge, expression shocky. "I have to get home."

"Adrian, no. There's no way to get there. I'll take you when it's safe." He found a turnaround, pulling off and crossing the bridge. "Right now, I'm taking you home, and we'll go from there."

"What? You can't! What about the code? What about my clothes?" The wolf was so close—almost brutally so—and Symon needed Adrian to pull it back. Neither of them needed to go fuzzy while driving.

"We'll set up a work area at my house. We'll have to go into the code through the back door, but I have that..."

Adrian turned those huge eyes on him. "You do?"

"Yes. I hired someone I trust to get in when I first bought the company. I didn't know you then."

"Who? You went out and creeped around in my code? Dude! You are not serious!"

"I am." He didn't point out that it was also his code. "Though to be fair, I never even looked at it. And my professional never touched anything. He just found a way in. I was concerned that the former owner might disable certain things when he left."

"No. That would be my department. I could do that, and I didn't because I rock like a rocking thing, and I have a moral code!"

"You do." He bit back a sigh. Adrian was freaking out, and he had every right. So he needed to be calm. Cool. Not furious that if Adrian had been home...

He hit the hands-free. "Call Cyrus." Time to check on Isaac again.

"Hey, boss. You okay? I'm heading to the office building."

"Have you heard?"

"I have a scanner. Mr. Kitty is being evacuated now."

"Okay. Get him somewhere safe. And I want this shit stopped. I'll have the onsite team account for everyone they can, but I don't like this one bit."

"No, neither do I, boss. I got this."

"And I have Adrian. We'll call back again as soon as you have Isaac."

"Got it." The connection clicked off, and he glanced at Adrian. "You're angry."

"Of course I am! You messed with my code. That's against all sorts of rules!"

"I appreciate that, baby, but I didn't mess with your

code. I just made sure I could recover it if something like this happened. And now I can and you have access."

"What about my apartment?" That was a tiny question that was so heavy.

"I'm pretty sure it's a lost cause, baby. But as soon as we can get someone in there, we will." Jesus, he was furious.

"I should have gone home. Maybe I could have stopped it."

"Or you could have been asleep when it happened." His gut churned. No, he wasn't going to think about that. Not one bit. If he did, his wolf would leap to the surface and he would go find someone and rip their throat out.

"But my stuff."

"We have your laptop. I know this is horrifying, baby. I would be—" He gritted his teeth. He would be able to replace anything he lost except family and Stan. So he needed to shut up. "You're not the kind to put your money in a mattress, right?"

"No." Adrian frowned at him as if that made no sense. "I have a diverse portfolio."

"Good." He pulled back on the highway, heading home. "Call Stan."

Stan answered on the first ring. "What's wrong?"

Stan always knew.

"Someone set fire to Adrian's apartment building."

"Oh my heavens. Is he all right? Wait, there's no way you were at work yet."

"Not even halfway. We're on our way back. Turn on the alarm. Cy has a guy headed our way, but I want you safe."

"Of course." He could hear the beep of the keypad as Stan turned on the security system. "I'll make soup and sandwiches. Poor Adrian has to be in awful shock."

He glanced sideways at Adrian, who was pale and still.

"I would say so, yes. Thanks, Stan. If you hear anything strange, go to the panic room."

"I will."

He hung up again, and Adrian blinked at him. "You have a panic room?"

"Mainly for Stan. He had a bad time of life before he met me. I want him to feel as though he has a place to hide."

"Oh." Now Adrian scowled deeply. "We won't let anyone hurt him."

"My thoughts exactly. I have one more call to make, okay?"

"Sure." Adrian stared out the window.

"Call Rian."

"Bro, this is what? Three times in a week?"

"I need you and Quin here."

Rian's voice went sharp. "What happened?"

"Another attack on the code. A fire at Adrian's building, which happens to be next door to the office. This is more than a disgruntled ex-employee."

"We can be there in four hours."

"Thank you." Quin's bar was in Aspen, so it would take them some time to get to him, but he was grateful.

"How's your little wolf?"

Adrian made a noise, shoulders hunching.

"Mad. Hurting. Upset as hell."

"Well, we'll kick ass and take names, I promise."

He bared his teeth. "That's the plan."

"Love you, bye."

"Love you."

"That's the lawyer?"

"Mmm."

"And Quin is..."

"The biker bar owner." He loved saying that, so much.

"Huh."

"You'll like him. He plays video games like you do."

"My consoles!" Adrian yelped. "Oh, my poor babies. I bet they're melted."

"Probably." He started a mental tally of all the things his mate would need replaced. "What all did you have?"

"PlayStation. Xbox. Switch. A classic Atari..."

"Shit, baby. I'm sorry." He reached over again. "I'll make it up to you. I swear."

"How?" Adrian crossed his arms over his chest, not letting him take a hand. "I mean, it's not like I had a bunch of family heirlooms, but my stuff was mine. And I worked hard for it!"

Symon knew Adrian wasn't shouting at him. He was just venting, so he let it happen, listening to Adrian's little howl with a wince. Fuck, this was a shitty situation. At least when he moved Adrian in with him, he knew Adrian liked his shower...

"And I don't have clean underwear or my shoes or my favorite hoodie! My pillows..."

"I know." He didn't, but it wasn't taking much to learn what Adrian valued. "You can wear one of my hoodies for now."

Adrian sniffed. "At least it will smell good."

That honored him, on a deep, abiding level. "Thank you."

The *mate* was implied.

Adrian shrugged. "It's true. And comforting. And I still want to cry."

"Of course you do. Not only did you potentially lose everything, it's possible someone was trying to do you harm." Wait. That wasn't super comforting, was it? "But you're going to be safe at the house until I figure this out."

"What if it was a random thing? Just an electrical thing."

He glanced sideways to meet Adrian's gaze. "Do you really think that?"

Adrian hunched back down in his seat. "No, of course not. But I don't want to think someone has it out for me."

"I understand." Symon and his brothers had been the target of corporate espionage-based violence more than once. It happened when someone did business at the level they did. But Adrian was just caught in the middle of a war he had no part in.

Adrian shrugged, then grabbed his phone and started searching.

"What are you looking for, baby?"

"My insurance stuff. I'll have to file a rental claim."

"I'll give you Rian's number. Text it to him and he'll take care of all of it." There was no need for Adrian to wear himself out dealing with all that stuff. Rian would get his replacement value in full.

"Oh, I wouldn't want to bother your brother."

"Eh. Quin will drive and he'll be bored." In no time, he was pulling back up at the house, and he studied it as he parked, making sure no one was lurking around.

"No one could be here, right? They're in Denver."

"Right. But I want to be sure no one went with divide and conquer." He had a feeling Adrian was right. If someone had been at Symon's place over the last few days, they would know Adrian was with him, not working from home.

Regardless, he wanted his pack together. All of them. The temptation to call all of them in was huge.

He took a deep breath. Okay, he needed to stop fretting

and get them inside. Protected. Safe. Then he would work on the rest.

"It's fine. Come on. I have work to do." There was an exhaustion in Adrian's voice, a deep sorrow.

They headed inside, and he put an arm around Adrian's shoulders to guide him. Adrian stiffened for a moment, but then leaned into him, shoulders hitching.

He didn't ask if Adrian was crying, and Adrian never let on, but he felt awful.

"Would you like to use my office, sweet? I can make the rest of my calls in the kitchen."

"Sure. You have good computers."

"I do." And they weren't connected to the work network unless he logged in through a secure connection his own team had set up for him. Not the Shiftr team.

"Good. I'll get this dealt with. Is there coffee?"

Stan came right to Adrian, grabbed him and held him tight. "People fucking suck."

Adrian sniffled, nodding against Stan's shirtfront. "They do. Especially big male cats who spray and act like it doesn't stink."

Stan chuckled, patting Adrian's back without letting go. "True enough. Big alphas of all kinds suck if they think they have a right to do whatever they want without repercussions." Stan glanced his way. "Some are more responsible than that."

"Are you sure?"

"Fairly certain. Would you like a cup of tea and some cookies?"

Adrian made a noise. "Oh. I need to work. But I love your cookies."

"Why don't we make the command center here in the kitchen? I can help. That way we can all eat our feelings."

Stan was a genius.

"Yeah?" Adrian snuffled.

"Absolutely. It's important to know you're around people that care."

"We do, baby. I'm not good at this stuff like Stan, but I want to be with you." He wanted to stand guard.

"Okay." Adrian pulled out his laptop to place it on the counter. "These are pretty comfy barstools." They had cushions and backs and all...

"Good. I'll make tea." Stan gave him a stern glance. "Sit down, Symon. Don't loom."

"I'm trying. My urge is to get all growly," he admitted, hoping it helped Adrian understand him.

"Alphas." Adrian rolled his eyes, but it wasn't mean. In fact, it was teasing, and it made him smile—almost.

He tugged out his phone to text Cy.

> Sitrep

I have Isaac

> Bring him here. Rian and Quin are on the way

Got it

Then he texted Rian.

> You on the way?

Yep. Making calls to ins reps.

> Excellent.

You warning the dads and all?

He shook his head.

The dickhead shouldn't care about the pack. This is business.

Got it. Be safe. We're making good time.

Yeah, he would bet they were. Quin could drive like the damn wind. Even in a car and not on a bike.

He put the phone down and put a hand on Adrian's legs as his omega's fingers flew on the keyboard. "Are you in?"

"I am. I'm working it." Adrian's head was down, lips tight together.

"Okay, baby. I'm right here if you need me." He knew Adrian well enough now to know he could work like this for hours on end, so he would be right there to make sure his omega drank tea and maybe juice, and ate things like cookies and fruit and turkey sandwiches.

"'Kay." Adrian lifted those gray eyes to his for a moment, showing he understood, the wolf flashing silver in them for a moment. "Thank you."

He nodded, then he started ordering clothes—hoodie, jeans, pajamas, shoes. Everything until Adrian could choose his own. He just needed Adrian to be outfitted...

A hoodie. He'd promised one of his, and he thought it would help Adrian settle in and feel comfortable. He moved out to the family room for a moment, grabbing one off the couch.

"Here, baby. I got you a hoodie. It's a little chilly in here."

Adrian took it from him and slid it on with hardly a glance his way.

He did hear, *Thank you. It's warm and it smells so good,* though.

You're welcome, baby. He squeezed one tense shoulder,

then slid over the tea that Stan set down. *You should try it. It's soothing.*

Yeah? Adrian grabbed the cup and took a sip. *Oh, yum.*

Good. It's my favorite too. That soothed him, down deep.

A smile curled Adrian's lips. *I can tell. I'm okay. I just need to work, to find out how they got in.*

Okay. I'm here. Don't hide from me too long. You'll need to rest before you meet my brothers. Rian and Quin could be a lot.

Adrian nodded, then shooed him. "Working."

He smiled a little, then moved to sit on his own stool and sip the coffee Stan gave him. He would do some work of his own.

Who knew how much time he'd have on his hands once the house was full.

CHAPTER

EIGHT

Adrian worked until the kitchen door flew open, and Isaac the wonder kitty came in, his scowl so deep his eyes almost disappeared.

"Adrian! Adrian, are you all right? They burned down your apartment!"

A tall man followed Isaac, grinning at him in a fond manner.

"I know. I don't know why, man. *We* didn't fire him!" He hugged Isaac hard. "Are you okay?"

"Fine. Seriously. Just fine." Isaac glanced at the wolf that followed him in, and whispered, "He keeps smiling at me."

"I think he likes you."

"I'm a kitty. He's a wolf."

"I didn't say he wanted to hit you up. Just that he likes you. You look like a grumpy kitty."

"Hmm. Is there any tuna?"

"There is." Stan beamed at Isaac. "I'm Stan. Would you like tea?"

"Oh, what kind? I love cardamom tea."

"I happen to have cardamom cinnamon."

"Yes, please."

"And a tuna sandwich."

"Would you like to make tuna salad? I have boiled eggs and celery."

Isaac nodded. "I'll totally do that for you."

"Very well." Stan moved around, and Isaac went to wash his hands, looking pretty relaxed for a cat in a wolf's den.

Then again, who could tell with Isaac? His expression never changed.

Adrian went back to work, repairing damage and settling everything back to right. He needed to make sure the damn code was stable, and then he'd start building in little bombs for anyone, who wasn't him or his two trusted guys at the troubleshooting department, that tried to get in and make changes. He would text them.

God, he hoped they were safe.

He sent them both encrypted messages, warning them about what was going on.

He got back panicky messages about the building being evacuated.

Yeah. Sucks. Stay safe.

Adrian hated that people were so...disrupted.

Over what?

Being fired?

You too

Dean told him. Poor guy. He was a nervy coyote shifter who had to be freaking out by now.

Will do.

He sighed softly and closed his laptop. His head was killing him.

"Hey." Symon pulled him close. "You get it figured out for now?"

"For now. I'm really tired."

"Do you want to go take a nap?"

"No. But can we all go sit in the family room and do something silly until your brothers show?"

"Absolutely."

"Wanna play a video game?" He wasn't going to be a bitch about all this. He wasn't.

"I do." Isaac munched tuna, the salad smelling strong but not bad. Clearly Isaac loved it.

It was just a little early for him to have tuna.

"Come on, baby. Let's go sit." Symon grabbed a plate of muffins in one arm, then his hand, taking him to the huge family room.

Isaac followed, glancing around curiously. "Dude. This is righteous."

"Thank you. Please, make yourself at home."

"Thanks." Isaac offered Symon what passed as a smile. "For everything."

"Of course." Symon sat close to him while Isaac munched and Stan passed out video game controllers. That was his and Isaac's jam, battling each other at some crazy game, and he noticed more than Mario Kart was now on tap. Someone had sent Stan shopping online in the days he'd been here.

The new wolf joined them, and they all started playing, and no one seemed to notice that he was tucked into Symon's side. Or maybe they didn't care.

Stan kept coming and going, bringing drinks and snacks, and they could smell wonderful scents coming from the kitchen as Stan cooked what he told them was lasagna when they asked.

"Do you need help?"

Stan wasn't a servant, was he? That would suck of Symon.

"No. No, this good, and there is help coming—Ben and Jamie are making a grocery run."

"Ben and Jamie?"

Symon rolled his eyes. "My cousin and his husband. They help out around here quite a bit."

"Oh." How had he not known that? But then, why would he? He knew very little about Symon, really.

"So do you have a whole pack?" Isaac asked curiously.

"I do. Most of them are up in Long's Peak, but we're wide-ranging."

"Who's the alpha?"

"My dad. Dad is still strong enough to hold the line, but I help whenever I need to, and so do Rian and Quin."

Oh, that made sense. A little. "I don't have a pack. I'm not pack-y." Adrian chuckled.

"Pack-y?" Isaac teased.

"Packish?" Adrian shot back.

"Packly?"

"Packadoodle?"

This was just hilarious.

"I'm lone." He shrugged.

"Not anymore," Symon murmured.

He wasn't sure what that meant, but pleasure suffused him.

It seemed amazing to feel as if he belonged, even if it

was a lie. He appreciated it, though, and he leaned on Symon, taking in his scent. So comforting.

Symon rumbled at him, nice and deep, and it echoed all the way down to the pit of his stomach. He let it buzz at the base of his skull, and he sighed, making Isaac grin over at him.

He'd been dozing for a long time when he woke to a flurry of activity, and Stan's voice sounded, clearly greeting newcomers.

He didn't know whether he needed to disappear or hide or what.

Symon held him right where he was, hand grasping his. "They'll come to us."

"Okay…"

"Brother!" A man who looked so much like Symon that it made him blink walked in first, coming to grab Symon up off the couch and hug him.

"Rian." Symon clapped him on the back. "This is Adrian. That's Isaac. And you know Cy."

"You're the lawyer, right?" Adrian asked.

"I am. You're the tech geek?"

"You know it."

"Welcome to the pack." Rian beamed at him, an evil little glint in his eye. He was way less serious than Symon. Adrian thought.

"I—thank you?" *Not pack.*

Are too.

Hush you. He poked Symon.

Nope. He's right.

Slower to follow, because he was chatting with Stan, was a long-haired man who was covered in tattoos and leather, his gaze taking in every detail of everything in the room.

"Ah, Quin. Out of jail?"

Quin bared his teeth. "Charges were dropped."

"Good. This is Adrian. Hands off, clear?"

Quin fastened him with a stare. "You want me to keep my hands off, puppy?"

Adrian glared over. "I've had a really shitty day, man. Don't. I'm not ready to joke around."

Quin's expression changed, going neutral. "I apologize. Tell us what's going on."

"They burned Adrian's apartment complex down. It's attached to the Shiftr building."

"Was it a personal attack?"

"We think so, yes." Symon kept talking, and he just let them all explain and rehash and revisit. He didn't want to listen to how he'd been a nice wolf and lost everything again.

Nope, he would just keep playing games with Isaac.

"I'm so sorry, Adrian," Rian said. "I'm on your insurance."

"Okay." He hunched up. "I'm not trying to be ungrateful, but could we change the subject for a bit?"

"Of course, baby. We can talk later once you turn in." Symon nudged his leg.

"Thank you. I just... I know it was nothing special, but it was mine." It had been his.

"Hey." Isaac glared at him. "It was special. It was your den. Don't ever apologize for being upset about that. My place is a one-room efficiency and I would lose it if someone torched it." His frown deepened. "Why am I here? Why am I not defending my lair?"

"Because you're not up to fighting that alone," Cy pointed out. "I have guys watching your place."

"I am more fierce than I appear..."

"I feel like you're pretty fierce, kitty." Cy gave Isaac a smile.

"I am. I have claws for days."

He had to grin at the byplay.

"What are we playing?" Rian, the suit, tossed his suit coat on the coffee table.

"Mario Kart. Grab a controller. Quin?"

"I want to go check out the fire damage. I'm going to head into the city. I'll be back."

"I could go," Adrian said. He needed to do something. He needed answers.

"You really couldn't." Quin gave him a sympathetic glance. "I'm better alone."

"But you don't know what you're looking for..."

"Oh, you'd be surprised." Quin winked at him. "I'm sort of morally flexible."

"Hmmm."

"That's an understatement," Symon murmured.

Quin winked at his brother. "Good thing you need me."

"I adore you, brat. Just don't get caught doing anything illegal."

"I'll do my best."

Quin headed out the door, the man disappearing like smoke.

Symon looked at Rian. "Is he okay?"

"He'll be fine. He's still mad." Rian took the game controller. "I, on the other hand, am ready to kick some ass."

"You'd better be better than your brother for that..." Isaac muttered.

"I am." Rian beamed.

Adrian chuckled, but he didn't care. He wanted Symon to hold him, that was all. And he got his wish, Symon cradling him against that broad chest while Isaac and Rian battled with go-karts onscreen. Oddly enough, he believed Quin would find out what had happened at his place.

Symon believed it, so it made it easy.

That and the smell of lasagna was super comforting.

With all of that in place, he could tell himself it would all be all right, even if only for a little while.

Now he just had to try to believe it.

CHAPTER

NINE

Symon carried Adrian to bed, trying not to worry.

He was, though. He was worried about Adrian, who was too quiet, so subdued. He was worried about Quin, who hadn't checked in yet, and it was pretty damn late.

And he was worried about what the next move would be. He had people searching for Carl and all his accomplices, but this seemed too...coordinated. Too big.

Adrian felt the same way.

This was about the business, possibly the pack. And he hated that Adrian had been dragged into this mess because of him.

But he wasn't willing to let Adrian go.

It wasn't an option, honestly. He needed his mate.

Dammit.

He laid Adrian on the mattress, smiling when his lover stirred, eyes opening. "Is it bedtime?"

"It is."

"I'm sorry. It's been a terrible day. I'm glad you were here."

"Me too. I'm so sorry you had to go through all this." He started tugging at Adrian's clothes, willing to just tuck him into bed, or to give more.

"Yeah." Adrian began to unbutton Symon's shirt as well, fingers hunting his skin.

Ah, so someone wanted comfort.

Good. So did he.

He stripped Adrian down gently, sliding his hands over all that lovely smooth flesh, searching out sensitive spots.

"I feel like I'm shaking apart, Symon," Adrian whispered.

"I want to help." He bent to kiss that sweet mouth nice and hard, pressing in with his tongue.

Adrian sobbed and opened up, letting him in deep. *Please.*

I have you, sweet. I do. I promise. He would give Adrian everything he had.

This whole thing had proven to him that he had things he was more concerned with than business or Zen. Adrian was the important part. The most important part.

He slid a hand down to Adrian's hip, gripping hard to pull them together.

Adrian didn't fight him at all. They melted together, their lips fastened to one another's. He pushed between Adrian's legs, spreading him, taking and giving the friction they both needed.

"Mmm." Adrian wrapped around him, holding him so close not even air could slide between them.

I've got you, mate. Just feel me. I have you. All of you.

I feel you. Please. More. I don't want to think.

He understood. *You don't have to, Adrian. Just let me love you.*

Love me. There was a wonder in that thought, and Adrian's eyes glowed a bright silver.

I swear it. He left it there for now, but god, he wanted to declare himself more strongly. He wanted Adrian with him, full stop. And he wanted everyone to know it. His brothers. Their coworkers. Well, maybe not their fired brethren. Them, he wanted to be in the dark.

Or possibly in a giant blazing fire.

That was a pleasant thought too. They deserved it for what they had done to Adrian.

"Stop thinking," Adrian groaned, hand behind his head to pull him in for another kiss, then another.

He moaned, pressing his thigh against Adrian's cock, letting him feel the pressure.

Adrian bit out a grunt, his toes curling, and that sweet prick leaked against him, easing the way.

"So hot for me." Was Adrian as hot inside? He dipped a finger down, sliding it in, and yes, Adrian was heated and wet and ready, squeezing down against him.

Ready to take his knot.

I need you. I'll take anything you have to offer. Anything you want. Adrian tossed his head, lips parted and hungry.

I want inside you, sweet. I want you to feel my knot. I want to ride you until we both scream. Symon gritted his teeth, pressing another finger inside Adrian, trying to wait until he knew his mate was ready for him. That was coming soon, he could tell.

Adrian nodded for him, hissing, "Now. Now is good."

Well, that was clear.

"Now is good," Symon agreed. He pressed his cock to Adrian's dripping hole, his body surging as he thrust in deep.

There was no hesitation, no resistance, just a huge heat.

And he pushed hard, his knot swelling immediately in response to the firm grip of Adrian's body.

Adrian moaned, lips parting as they shivered.

"So damn pretty, love. I could kiss you all day. Touch you like this."

"Good. I need it. You. This."

"I'll help make it better. I promise." He licked at Adrian's lips, then kissed him again. Helping him lose himself.

Adrian smiled, the expression wondering as they made love. They rocked together, and Adrian touched his cheek, fingers hot and gentle, the caress making him lose his breath.

He growled softly, his world spinning. Gods, he could just forget everything else and love Adrian. Seriously. Everything else faded away in sight of him.

Everything else. Yours. Yours, Symon. The thought almost stopped his heart.

I want that. Adrian. Mate. There. He'd said it. Not out loud, but where it mattered. So it was real.

Those silver eyes flashed, and for a moment, they were running together, hard and fast. Under the moon. It was the headiest feeling he could ever remember, and his knot lodged deep.

Adrian held onto him, fingers digging into his shoulders. They were so close now they might as well have been one being. And soon they would both spend together.

And then I will hold you all night, he promised.

Yes. Please. I need you. Adrian clung to him, panting, body thrumming with desire and pleasure. *I swore I'd never be an alpha's, but you—*

Mine. You're mine now, love. And I swore I would never get all wolfy...

And I can see him, your wolf.

I can see yours. They're running together.

And they were loving each other as well. He'd never felt this, where they were both animal and man. And he wanted to feel it again, over and over. He wanted to give Adrian this all the time.

He wanted to come hard and often, feeling Adrian's squeezing heat all around him.

Adrian clawed at his back. "Now. Please. So close."

"Right here." He reached for Adrian's cock, stroking hard.

"Yes!" Adrian bowed so hard he felt like he might snap in two, and he clamped down on Symon so hard that Symon came, his knot fully engaged, throbbing and sending lightning up his spine.

Adrian blinked up at him, that silver clear and shining like the moon.

He understood the call of it now. He and his wolf felt...at home. Together.

No yoga needed.

TEN

Adrian woke up in the dark hours of the morning and headed out to the kitchen to find coffee. Maybe a snack. He wasn't sure. He required a certain amount of flaky pastry in his life.

He yawned, pulling the fluffy robe he'd used before around him, his feet swathed in socks that were far too big. The scent of coffee reached him, and he geared up to smile at Stan, but it wasn't Stan at all.

It was the long-haired biker brother. Quaid? Quist?

Quin.

"Hey. Uh. Sorry. I need coffee."

"No worries. I bought early-morning doughnuts on the way back in from Denver." The smile was so much like Symon's, but held a wild edge. Quin dipped his chin and grabbed a second mug. "Coffee is a necessary evil."

"Oh, it's not evil. It's so yummy." He took the cup once Quin poured, then added cream and sugar.

"Yeah. So, why are you in my brother's bed?"

"Huh?" He choked on some coffee, almost spitting it out.

"You heard me. Your apartment is torched. Your department was attacked. You're seducing Symon. Even if it's not evil, it's connected. So, talk to me."

"I—We met at work. I'm the lead software guy on the app..." He shrugged. "He's hot as hell. And he called to me."

"So...is there something creepy with the code?"

"Creepy how?" Code was ones and zeroes. No creep factor.

"I mean, is it skewed somehow? Does it collect sensitive information? Beam radiation from space?"

"Uh... I'm pretty sure it gathers information to make sure ads get to the interested parties and that's it?"

"Huh." Quin studied him like he was a bug under a magnifying glass. "So what's the deal with people setting your shit on fire?"

"I don't know. I mean, Isaac and I stood up to Carl, but you don't burn someone's apartment up for that!"

"No, you don't." Quin sipped his coffee. "So what's going on? What do you know about this Carl guy?"

"He's a mountain lion. He's mean. He hates Isaac?"

"Hmmm." Quin tapped his fingers against his cup. "You think this is a sex thing?"

"Like with me? Ew! No!" Gag. No felines.

"No, I mean with this Carl guy and your friend Isaac. And you're a friend of Isaac's, you defended him... Right? I think Rian told me that."

"Maybe? But then why keep attacking the app?" Isaac worked in the damn mail room, for goodness sake. "And the code that they're messing with—it's just slowing things down, causing glitches. If you're going to attack, why not a DOS attack or steal personal information. This is more a drama of gradually escalating irritation."

"Then who besides your old boss would have a vested interest in the app failing?"

"Quin, are you torturing my mate?" Symon walked in with the lawyer, Rian, both of them in pajama pants and sweaters. "Did you get doughnuts?"

"I did, yeah. A couple dozen."

"Good man." Symon kissed his neck, then went to pour a cup of coffee. "Adrian isn't the bad guy here."

"I never accused him of that, did I?" Quin fastened him with a glare, and Adrian shook his head.

"No. No, he said I was involved somehow, but he never said I was at fault, you know?" Even if it felt like it a little bit.

"No one here is at fault for anything." Symon said it in a firm voice, touching his back. "This is an attack—on you, on me, on the company—and I am going to quash it."

Growly Symon was kind of hot.

"Sexay," Rian said, that wolfish grin so like Quin's, only in a lawyer kind of way.

"Gross." Quin rolled his eyes. "And I'm in. I just want answers."

"So do I." Adrian puffed up a little, because he couldn't help it. "My stuff is all gone. All of it. And for what?" He shook his head. "I mean, come on. I just wanted a cup of coffee and a snack. I didn't ask for any of this."

"Of course not." Rian nodded at him. "Don't let Quin make things weird. He's just a hard ass."

"And a champion of the underdog." Symon glared at Quin. "So clearly he's just fucking with you."

"Hey, I want to make sure he's not messing with you, bro. You come first." Quin shrugged, not the least bit guilty, he thought.

Adrian sighed. Of course Symon came first. He always

came second, and he had a headache. He stood and shook his head. "I'm going to take a shower before I get back to work."

"I'll come with you." Symon snagged a bunch of doughnuts, then walked with him toward the bedrooms. "I'm sorry about them, love."

"They're your brothers, your pack. It's only right."

"That they worry about me? Yes. That Quin was rude to you? No." Symon nudged him with one arm, hands too full of pastry to touch him.

"No?" He stole a doughnut, tore off a bite, and fed it to Symon as they walked.

"Mmm. Maple." Symon chuckled, chewing. Then he swallowed. "And no. No one gets to be mean to you."

"Well... I... Really?" That made him all shivery and dry mouthed.

"Really." Symon nudged open the bedroom door, and he closed it behind them while Symon put the doughnuts down on the night table. "Come eat with me."

"Okay. I'm sorry." He wasn't absolutely sure what he was sorry for, but he was totally sorry.

"Why?" Symon tempted him with a bite torn off a blueberry lemon doughnut.

"Oh, thank you. I don't know, mate. I feel... responsible."

"Well, then maybe you know something you don't think you know."

Adrian tilted his head. "Is that a thing?"

"Yes. When Rian was still doing trials, he often said a witness who had seen more than they actually recalled would often have a feeling of guilt. Maybe you saw someone doing something that didn't twig you at the time..."

"Really? Do you think I saw stuff? I was always in the code..."

"Maybe. And Isaac. He's at the office earlier than anyone else. What if he saw something too? Something he didn't know to parse as bad acting." Symon munched half a jelly doughnut.

"Maybe. I mean, Carl's a bully and a dick. He was always trying to intimidate Mr. Lepus, to get promotions, to get more."

"Hmmm. I'll put Rian on his background and acquaintances."

Adrian shrugged. "He's a salesman, you know? You can't really trust anything to be absolutely true."

"No lies detected." Symon winked at him. "Come on. Have another bite or two and we'll take a shower."

"Can I have one of the crullers? I love those."

"Of course." Symon handed it over, then licked his fingers.

"Thank you." He took a bite, humming under his breath. "Oh, fresh."

"Mmmhmm. Quin has good taste in doughnut places." Symon sighed. "I'm not sorry. I wouldn't have gotten to have you if this hadn't happened. The sale, I mean. Not the drama."

"Lepus wanted out. He wanted to be on a yacht on the open ocean. He was tired of the drama." And Adrian got it— he was a coder. He didn't do things.

"Well, he got out. But what did Carl think he was getting?" Symon ate another doughnut. "Ready for that shower?"

He nodded and stood. "He couldn't have bought the company. He's in management. He sells shit."

"So what if that's not what he wanted?" Symon drew

him to the bathroom. "What if he was stealing? Money. Code. Something. What if all these little annoyances are to cover his tracks while he tries to get in and get more?" Symon sounded thoughtful. And dangerously calm.

He shivered. He wouldn't want to get on Symon's bad side.

Still...it wasn't...

He tilted his head, blinking. "He's a salesman. He sells things. He's good at it."

"Mmmhmm." Symon said it encouragingly.

"What if he was trying to sell the code to a competitor?"

"And then you and your team keep changing things, so he has to keep trying to get the full code?"

"Yeah, it was insane, because they kept pushing us to improve, to make the sale sweeter, you know?" They'd all been working sixteen-hour days.

"That's got to be it." Symon closed his eyes. "I passed that on to Rian," he said a few moments later. "Let him start looking into it." He turned on the water, and steam started pouring out almost immediately.

He was beginning to be addicted to this shower. He knew that he was bound to Symon, but this bathtub was a huge bonus...

Symon laughed. "You just love me for my rainbath."

"And your doughnuts. And your Wi-Fi is mind-blowing."

"Why thank you. So is my knot, hmm?"

He flushed hot, still not used to hearing things, or saying things, like that, even though Symon inspired him. "So true. That's a work of art."

"I'm glad you think so."

"It makes my mouth dry, you know? You make me dizzy."

"You do the same for me." Symon kissed him, stripping them both before pushing him into the spray. "And I want to do bad things to you all the time. Like it distracts me from everything else."

"That's the mate bond forming, right?"

"I suppose so." Symon stroked his hair. "I hope it never fades at all."

"I understand now why people crave this." Adrian leaned toward his mate. "Why wolves crave this."

"Yes. I know what you mean." Symon pulled him close and held him, washing him with lazy strokes.

Adrian leaned hard, eyelids heavy, his tension disappearing with a pop. He wanted to rest. To go back to sleep. He wanted other things too, but it wasn't urgent right now. It could wait.

Everything could, because he had Symon in his arms.

ELEVEN

Symon left Adrian sleeping again rather than working, and he went out to get another cup of coffee, find some protein, and bitch at his brothers about being assholes and tell them about what he and Adrian had discussed.

He thought they might be onto something, and he really wanted to get the ball rolling on Carl and any of his possible accomplices. If they had even part of the code promised to someone else, they needed to be stopped. And they were officially in criminal territory with the fire now.

"Quin's in bed, so you can rail at me, okay?" Rian shook his head. "He was just protecting you."

"I know. But Adrian didn't deserve the grilling. You know that."

"I can see it, sure. But I was a criminal lawyer for a while. I know the look. And Quin is hot-headed." Rian tilted his head. "You have an idea. I can see it. Any new information on what's going on?"

"This Carl guy. I think he was trying to steal the code and sell it. The little bombs he's setting off inside the app are covering his tracks. And I think somehow both Isaac and Adrian know something they shouldn't." He thought Carl had chosen them to pick on at the welcome event to goad them into talking. But they had no idea they had anything to talk about.

"Like what? What are they holding back?"

Symon shook his head. "Nothing that I know of, but I don't think they know either."

"So Carl knows they saw something, but those two don't realize what it is..." Rian nodded. "I can buy that. And he had to be surprised, thinking he'd gotten away with it, and then you fired him."

"Yes." Symon nodded. "Adrian and his team keep changing the code and the passwords and all, so he doesn't have it all."

"So he burned the apartment to get Adrian there? To get the code?"

"I don't know. Maybe both. Maybe neither. Maybe he's just in a fury at this point. But I would bet he's looking for both of them..." Carl had to know both Isaac and Adrian were gone by now.

"Excellent. Well... I vote we find this son of a bitch and deal with him." Rian's growl was clear as a bell.

"I think that's a good idea. And any accomplices too." He wasn't the hunt-them-down-and-kick-ass type, but he was feeling...wolfy about this.

Rian's eyebrow lifted. "Mmm...yummy. We're in."

"You're an ass. Just like Quin."

"Nope. I find motorcycles wicked uncomfortable."

"I need to leave someone besides Stan here with Isaac and Adrian. Cy?"

"Cy, and we'll bring another couple. It takes a pack to take down a mountain lion."

"It does, and he's not alone. So we'll make sure it's safe." He took a deep breath. "Quin will be so pleased."

"Yeah. So you want to go now, see if we can find our arsonist?"

"I do. Let's get Quin." He would also alert Cy.

"Sounds like a plan. I'm going to call in my people, as well."

"Thanks, brother. Do you think we need to warn Dad?"

"I think there will be hell to pay if we don't."

"I bet you're right. Okay. Get Quin. I'll call Dad and get Cy. Meet you at the garage." He needed more tactical clothing than he had on as well.

Adrian was still dozing, curled in a ball in his bed, holding his pillow and snuggling it. Symon caught himself standing there, drinking in the sight of his mate like Adrian was fine wine.

He took a deep breath, reminding himself that he was doing this not just to keep his business safe, but to make sure any threat to his mate was neutralized.

Adrian's eyes opened. "Mate? What's wrong?"

This was not on his bingo card. He'd needed Adrian to stay asleep.

Maybe you shouldn't have stood there and stared at him, that voice in his head piped up.

"Nothing, love. I'm going to run out with Rian and Quin for a bit. You and Isaac need to stay here with Cy and Stan, okay?" He knew Adrian would argue. That independent stubbornness was one of the best things about him. But it could be sticky right now.

"Are you going to hunt for Carl? Do you think you'll be able to find him? I can help."

"How, baby?" He wasn't dismissing the claim. He just wanted to hear what Adrian's thoughts were.

"Well, he wants the code, doesn't he? I can try to call him, sound desperate, ask him to sell it for me."

That made him pause. "Do you think he'd believe it?"

"Why wouldn't he? My whole apartment is trashed. The big cats are territorial, so he might be working alone, but one way or another if he's already made the sale, he's more desperate than I am. That makes people stupid."

"Hmm." He tapped his finger against his lower lip. "Maybe if you tell him I brought you home for a fling and then dumped you..."

"Do you think he knows I'm here?"

"I bet he knows you're with me somewhere. We didn't make a secret of it."

"Then he knows where Isaac is too..."

"He might speculate on that, but Cy did some skullduggery when he went to get Isaac... I think it's the best story we have." He gave Adrian a look. "If you really want to help."

"Why wouldn't I? That's how this whole thing started. Just because you can be an asshole doesn't give you the right to do it."

"Oh, baby, I didn't mean that. I just mean it might be dangerous, and I prefer you safe, but I would never order you to do anything." He would never take away Adrian's agency that way, even if the alpha in him wanted to growl and demand.

Now, he might limit Adrian's actual contact with anyone in Carl's circle, but he wouldn't mention that.

Adrian snorted. "You could try. I'm my own wolf. If I do as you ask, it's because I want to. It's my gift to you."

"Exactly." He grinned when Adrian laughed. "Okay, then. Get dressed, baby. We've got a mountain lion to catch."

"I'll wear the clothes I came in. My choices are limited." Adrian nodded to him. "My laptop is charged. I'm ready to do this."

"Okay. You have clothes on the way, as far as that goes. Then we'll go shopping." He led Adrian to the garage. The car had Wi-Fi. Adrian could make his offer from there.

"Sounds good. Is someone staying to protect Isaac?"

"Cy will stay. Stan is here. And Rian called in some of his people too."

Rian turned when they walked into the garage, eyebrows going up. "He's coming?"

"I am. I'm going to contact Carl and set up a meeting." His omega was adorable.

"I think he can draw the guy out."

Quin came in, decked out for battle. "Well, then, we'll take the help. But if shit hits the fan, you duck and cover."

"I'm not interested in getting disemboweled, thanks," Adrian shot back. "I have future plans."

Lord, he loved Adrian so much already. So cute when he was deadpan.

Quin actually chuckled. "Or beheaded? Good deal."

"Symon wants me for my brain, you know."

"I know."

"And your body. The whole package." Symon patted his butt, but then sobered. "You're my mate. I want you, full stop."

"Guys. Gag. Just stop. No one needs to hear that shit." Rian rolled his eyes while Quin gagged dramatically.

"Oh, like you wouldn't make me listen to it." Symon opened the car door and motioned him in.

"You don't get carsick, do you?" Quin asked.

"What? I'm not a puppy!" Adrian glared at Quin. "You need to back off. I'm not here to hurt your big brother."

"I just meant I intend to drive fast, and you'll be working." Quin held up his hands. He did respect people more if they stood up to him, and Symon was super proud.

"Oh. Sorry. No, I don't have a nausea problem." Adrian offered Quin a smile. "Truce?"

"Truce." Quin winked, and Symon was used to that making people blush. Not his mate, though. Adrian sat down, opened his laptop, and got to work.

Quin arched an eyebrow, but the expression was completely approving.

"Come on, you lot," Rian said. "Let's get this done. I want to know my investment is safe."

"It is." Symon just needed to know his mate was safe.

CHAPTER

TWELVE

Rumor is you can sell things for a
commission.

Who this?

Adrian allowed himself a smile.

U know who I am

He just needed to dangle his wormy hook a little.

And I don't believe you want to sell

"Fucker."

I don't want to, asshole. I have to. There
was a big boom at my apt.

well, run to the new boss and blow him

been there, done that. U want the code or not? U have 10 secs before I go somewhere else and u can fuck off

I want it.

Score. He was setting the hook. "He wants it. How much do I ask for?"

"Well, I bought the company for a lot of millions..." Symon grinned. "But crimes like this tend to be quick and dirty. A couple hundred thousand?"

"No. Don't go too low. Ask for ten million." Quin sounded so sure. "Let him barter you down, sure, but ask high."

Adrian's eyebrows shot up. "Are you sure?"

"Yes. You wrote this code. You're not just some corporate raider with no connection to it. He needs to believe you're emotional."

"Okay. I can see that." Adrian tapped away.

10 Mil

No fucking way

it's worth 10x that & u know it

He just had to set up a meeting. That was it. Just a meeting.

Not to me. I just want a clean copy. You can sell it to as many people as you want. 2 mil.

He almost dropped his laptop. Holy shit.

"What? What is it?" Symon asked, and he met those beautiful eyes.

"He just wants a copy. He's offering two million dollars. What do I do?"

"Say yes," Rian said. "We're just drawing him to a meeting. Tell him you don't want an electronic payment. You want to meet with him."

"He won't be suspicious?"

"How techie is he?"

"Not at all, as far as I know. He's a salesman."

"Tell him you need cash to get out of town," Quin said. "That you're scared of Symon's pack."

"I can totally do that." He grabbed his laptop and typed in,

> You got it. Where do we meet?

> What do you mean meet?

> You know, meeting that thing that two people do when one of them is going to hand over $2,000,000 and the other one is going to hand over stolen code?

Adrian had to admit that this was really, truly kind of a powerful position to be in. He wasn't sure he liked it. But it was good to know about himself—whether or not he could do this.

> I'll wire you the money. U send the code.

Adrian shook his head.

> No. I do not think so. I have to get out of town. Do you think that the pack won't hunt me down once they find out what I've done? I want cash. And I want it now.

I have to meet with my buyer first.

Fair enough. Will an hour work?

Adrian could almost feel Carl's panic through the computer. It was literally a palpable thing. He was glad. Fucker. He deserved it.

I can do an hour

Where? I'm downtown.

Meet me in the park in front of the Science Museum

cuin60

"He wants to meet in the park by the Science Museum in an hour."

"We can be there." Quin slid out on the highway and picked up speed.

"So, what do I do? What do you need from me? What am I supposed to do?"

"Your job is done, baby." Symon stroked his arm. "You did great. The rest you leave to us."

"Really? I did a good job? Do I have to meet him?"

"No. No, he'll be there, and we'll see him before he realizes he didn't see you. We have the texts as his intent to buy."

Quin scoffed. "I don't intend to take him to the police."

"Just don't get hurt. I—You're—we just started. Please don't get hurt."

"I won't. I'll toss Quin in the way of his claws."

He wasn't sure if he was supposed to laugh, but Rian did, so he grinned. "Okay."

"Hey!"

"The leather jacket will protect you, right?" he dared to tease.

"Yeah, yeah. That and Rian when I use him as a shield."

"Ah, brotherly love," Rian said, rolling his eyes at him and Symon in the back seat. "Do you have a big family?"

"No. No, not at all." He was a loner, no question.

"Well, welcome to ours then."

He blinked hard, not with confusion this time, but with emotion. "Thanks. That's— thanks."

Symon rumbled softly, stroking his back. *Easy, mate. All is well.*

I know. I do. I worry about you, but I know. And your brothers are sweet.

Oh now, don't go too far. But they do accept that you have my best interest at heart.

I do. So quickly, so wildly—you call to my soul.

I feel the same.

"Are you two making googly eyes? Focus, Symon." It wasn't long before Quin was pulling off the highway in Denver and heading toward the downtown museum area.

Adrian could feel the mixture of apprehension and excitement from the brothers, and it made him queasy.

Symon pressed his hand. *It will be fine. There are enough of us to take on a cat.*

I'm here too. If you need me. I won't leave you unprotected.

I know that. And I love you for it. But I want you to try to stay down and wait until it's absolutely necessary. I might get distracted worrying about you.

That's fair. He understood that, 100 percent. He would be smart, but he wouldn't let anyone hurt Symon.

He would fight for his mate, just as his mate was fighting for him.

"Okay. We're almost there," Quin said. "Everyone on

alert."

"He doesn't know you, Quin. Can you head out, let us know what you see?"

"Sure, Sy. I can play drunken asshole number two, no sweat."

"Good man. You know what he looks like?"

"I memorized the pics, yeah." Quin coasted to the most crowded area of the parking lot. This part of Denver was never fully dead. "Cover me, Ri."

"I got you." Rian pulled a heavy sweater on, which made him look softer and more bulky.

He slumped down, hiding in the shadows of the back seat. "This is wild. You guys be—"

Quin slipped out of the car, and Adrian noticed the interior light didn't come on. Neat trick.

Rian gave them a wicked grin in the rearview, then did the same, waving one hand.

Symon stayed with him, sitting back in the shadows, watching everything from the car window.

"Are you okay?" he whispered.

"I'm pissed off. Someone wants to harm my mate."

He poked Symon's leg. "They want to hurt mine too."

"Yes, but I think Carl blames you very personally for the fact that he hasn't been able to get what he wants. I want to chew him up and spit him out."

"Yeah, I want him to go away. I just want to have a life with a rhythm again. It's hard to be floating around like a chicken with its head cut off."

"I know." Symon didn't look at him, but he felt that hand press his. "I hope you want to make a new routine with me."

"I hope you want the same thing," he whispered. "I want to be with you."

"I want you too, love. I tell myself I'm not wolfy, but you make me want to claim you. To mate you so good you never leave me."

"That sounds...delicious." But first they had to focus on getting Carl.

"It does. There he is." He felt Symon tense, and then the pressure seemed to grow inside the car. He got the feeling Symon was communicating with his brothers.

"Are they okay?" he whispered. He wanted to hide, but he needed to protect his pack—whether or not it was his yet.

"They will be. I just wanted them to know I'd spotted him. Quin will move in and distract him." Symon vibrated, and he could tell his mate wanted to be out there, working with his brothers, keeping them safe as they kept him that way.

He saw Carl then, and his stomach turned. The man was really ugly somehow. Like he had an aura of badness.

"Dammit, Adrian! Where are you?" Symon heard the son of a bitch even through the closed windows.

I can go out there if I need to.

No. Symon held him close. *No, Quin is closing in.*

Adrian heard Quin singing at the top of his lungs, stumbling around and making a ton of noise. It was a little hilarious, honestly, and more than a touch impressive.

Rian was moving in from behind Carl, and he could tell the moment Carl knew he was had. He whirled toward Rian, and Quin rushed at him from behind, and Symon slid out of the car with barely a breeze in his wake.

Adrian stashed his laptop under the seat and grabbed his phone. He probably should dial nine and one.

He held his breath, watching as Quin took Carl down, but he was surprisingly strong for such a doughy-looking guy, twisting hard and tossing Quin off.

Everything stopped when Carl pulled out a gun.

Adrian grabbed his empty laptop bag, slipped out of the passenger side, and then stood up. "What the fuck? You brought backup?"

"Are you kidding? Like I was going to trust a fucking wolf. And I was right, wasn't I?" Carl sneered at him.

"Who are these two assholes that you brought? I told you I was coming! You're just a prick! You are a hateful piece of shit!" He was screaming now, hoping to confuse and distract Carl for the brothers.

"What the fuck?" Carl actually backed away from him. "You've fucking lost it."

"You burned down my apartment! You are a BAD KITTY!"

This was actually cathartic.

"Of course I am. Give me the laptop, Adrian." Carl's hand was starting to shake, and he kept darting glances at Symon and his brothers.

"You cheated. You brought wolves! You know I'm a solitary wolf! You CHEATED ME!" He threw his head back and howled, the wolf in him demanding to be let out.

And that startled Carl enough that he lowered the gun, and that was all it took. Quin took him down again, Symon kicking the gun away while Rian landed a hard blow to Carl's chest, winding him. And in moments, Quin and Symon had him tied up.

"Who else is in on it with you, Carl?" Symon snapped.

"Fuck you!"

"No." Adrian growled, storming over to pop Carl in the jaw. Hard. "Tell him, you fuckmonkey!"

"Your mate is a scrapper, Sy," Quin murmured.

"I know." Symon gave him a look that warmed him to

CHAPTER

THIRTEEN

Symon walked the halls of the house, the need to make sure everyone was locked in safely strong. His alpha nature made him wish to protect everyone, even his brothers, though Quin was still out there looking for Carl's accessory to crime, Henry Gaines.

He would bet almost anything that Quin would find the guy before the cops did.

Isaac, Cy, and Stan had gone to bed a while ago, and Adrian was still tapping away at his computer, so it was Rian who met him in the kitchen when he went to make hot chocolate. They had already eaten all the Insomnia cookies he'd ordered.

"Dad will be here in the late morning."

"Oh, Lord. I forgot we called him."

Rian chuckled, sitting on a stool and watching him heat up milk. "Yeah. He's super curious to meet your mate."

"Yay." Symon wrinkled his nose. "Okay, that sounds bitchy. I need Dad to meet him anyway, right?"

"Yep. That's the easy gateway into the pack."

Chuckling, he waited for bubbles to form on top of the

milk so he could stir in the white chocolate. They all tolerated that better than milk or dark. "You guys were his trial by fire."

"True enough." Rian tapped his fingers on the counter. "So how big of a problem do you think this app thing is actually going to be?"

"Well, I certainly never thought Shiftr was going to be more than a niche market. So maybe we need to look deeper at what the bunny was up to."

"Okay, can you delve there? That way my fingers aren't in it."

"Sure. I'll get Quin on it too. He can do in-person inquiries and I'll make calls and do deep dives online. Did Adrian ever figure out what he saw?"

"No, and neither did Isaac, but it had to be important."

"Hmm. Well, stay on it," Rian told him.

"I will." In fact, as soon as he made the hot cocoa he was going to take some to Adrian and shut him down for a while, most likely by loving him into a puddle.

They all deserved some downtime, and he knew Adrian's nerves were shot.

Adrian had bags under his eyes big enough to pack enough to take a three-week-long trip, and he thought his mate didn't even know he was crying, although tears streaked his cheeks.

Sweet baby.

He headed over and growled, "Hit save."

"What? I don't know what you mean."

Symon looked at him, glared a little bit, and said, "You do too."

His poor omega was at the end of his rope, and Symon understood that. He was feeling like he was clinging to the edges himself. Still, it was the alpha's job.

To his credit, Adrian did hit save, right before Symon shut the cover of the laptop.

Then he just picked Adrian up and headed toward the bedroom. The crisis—this crisis—so far had been averted. And it was time to just be with his mate.

After all, his fucking father was going to be there in the morning.

Adrian wrapped both arms around his neck. "Today was the weirdest day of my life. And that is in a life of admittedly fucking odd days."

"I know." He did know. He'd dealt with corporate espionage before, but nothing like this.

"I know you know." Adrian shook his head. "Still, I cannot believe this. This is stupid." Adrian stared at Symon like he was trying to express an emotion that he didn't even understand himself. "This code wasn't worth that much, what he was willing to sell it for was not worth that much. You could hire someone or a bunch of someones, and it would take time sure, but—damn it. I don't understand. Part of the—a big part of it—of this company's value is in its reputation, not the code. Anybody can write code."

"No. No that's not entirely true, love." He kissed Adrian's neck. "You have a spark for it. You and your team. Even Helene says so. And I looked at half a dozen buy-out possibilities, but Shiftr was the best because it was so intuitive for the end user."

Adrian blinked at him, wide-eyed. "I think that's the nicest thing anyone's ever said to me, ever since, like, the beginning of time."

Symon wasn't sure if that was the most adorable or the saddest thing he'd ever heard in his entire life. He was going to go with adorable, because he had said it, so he got the credit for it, but still. Damn.

"Well, it's true." He turned so Adrian could open the bedroom door for them. "And I thought that before I ever saw you."

"Are you saying you wanted me for my code, Symon?"

"I did. And now I want you in all ways. As my mate." He placed Adrian gently on the bed. No tossing today. It had already been jarring enough.

"And I want you to hold me. My head hurts."

"Of course." He stripped down, then crawled into bed and grabbed Adrian in his arms, pulling the blanket over them. "I'm right here."

"I know. I'm sorry. I'm being a weenie, it's just... He had a gun." Adrian squeezed his eyes shut tight, snuggled in closer. "That was super scary. I was convinced he was going to shoot you, hurt you or one of your brothers. I just... I panicked."

"If that was panic, go you." Adrian had done well, even if he'd put himself in danger.

"I tried. But you had told me to stay in the car, and I was worried I'd make you mad, and then he was such a dick, and I was so scared for you..."

"And I lost a year off my life when he pointed the gun at you," Symon said.

"I understand. I totally understand, but there wasn't anything I could do. All I could think was that he had a gun and that you guys were going to get hurt. So I figured I'd just bluff my way out of it and try to distract him long enough to let you do what it was that you were there to do." Adrian's face burned where it touched Symon's chest. "I mean, seriously. I didn't even let myself think. If I had, I would have screwed it up. I know I would have, but all I could think was that my mate was out there, and I couldn't just let things happen."

Symon let that sink in a second.

He was the eldest child. He was the one in line to lead the pack once his father stepped down. He was the protector.

And while he knew that his brothers always had his back, unquestioningly, there was something amazing about the fact that he was someone's first thought.

He just rumbled, letting Adrian hear it, hoping it would soothe him. There was something soul-satisfying about holding him, knowing Adrian needed him, that they needed each other.

Adrian immediately relaxed, easing into him with a sigh.

"That's it, sweet. That's perfect." Symon let himself relax as well.

"It is perfect, you know." He could feel Adrian melt and rest. Just let go and trust.

In him.

Not only was it an amazing feeling, but his wolf insisted.

This was right.

FOURTEEN

Adrian was on his fourth cup of coffee when he heard this booming voice, ringing from the front room of the house.

"Where is that boy?"

Stan murmured an answer, but Adrian didn't exactly hear it.

He couldn't.

Everything in him stilled suddenly, and he needed to run. He wasn't sure whether or not his instinct was to run toward the voice or away, though. So he sat there sort of frozen, like some panicked little rabbit, which was weird because he liked rabbits.

He'd had a rabbit boss. He knew rabbits socially.

Symon, on the other hand, didn't seem to be having the same problem. He just rolled his eyes. "It's Dad."

Yeah, Adrian sort of figured.

Rian and Quin were still in bed, of course, and not here to help Symon with their father.

Adrian assumed that, when you were second-in-command of an entire pack, you were expected to be awake and functional once your father showed up.

He wouldn't know.

"Should I go? Wait in the other room?"

Symon rolled his eyes. "Don't. Just don't. His bark is worse than his bite."

"What did you say, boy?"

Suddenly, Adrian could see exactly what Symon was going to look like in thirty years—big, beautiful, silver, completely convinced of his own power. This man was effortlessly alpha.

"I said your bark was worse than your bite, old man." Symon stood up. Meeting him chest to chest, their eyes locked.

Adrian was fairly sure he was going to pee himself any moment.

Then Symon's father roared with laughter and grabbed Symon in a hard hug, clapping him on the back several times.

Symon laughed too, squeezing his dad in a way that might have broken Adrian's bones.

"Good to see you, son."

"You too, Dad. Thanks for coming to check on us."

"Mmm. Who's the little omega?"

"Mine." Symon blinked like he'd just confused himself. "I mean, this is my mate, Adrian. Adrian, Thomas, my dad, the head of the Boulder River pack. Dad, this is Adrian."

Adrian stood and held out one hand, and he was pretty proud of himself because it wasn't shaking too bad.

And he wasn't hyperventilating too much.

Basically, he was a great.

Totally not intimidated, completely not about to cry, because that would be bad.

"Pleased to meet you, sir."

Go team him.

"Your mate." Thomas looked at Symon with wide eyes. "You didn't tell me that you were pursuing a mate."

Symon shrugged. "I know I didn't. I mean, I didn't know. That I was... This is very new and sudden." Symon looked over at him and smiled. "But welcome. Completely and totally welcome."

"Well, okay then." Thomas sat, and immediately Stan was there with coffee and a cinnamon roll the size of his head. When Thomas looked over at Stan, it was with a gentle, completely nonthreatening expression, the big alpha seeming incredibly careful. "Which pack are you from?" he asked Adrian. "I'd like to contact them and make our greetings."

Oh man, that was a can of worms. Adrian went with the simplest, truest possible answer. "I don't have a pack. I'm a solitary."

"Okay, but where did you come from?"

"I hatched from an egg." He wasn't doing this. "It was a big egg."

One silver eyebrow winged up. "It wasn't that big."

"Dad, stop. He's his own wolf, okay? Well, and now he's part of our pack. That's all we need to know." Symon reached for him, and he took that hand like a lifeline.

He held on tight, breathing, letting Symon's strength really bolster him. In his experience, big alphas could be a real nightmare, so he had to work to keep his shit together.

"All right. All right, I just wanted to welcome your omega to our family. I meant no disrespect." Thomas backed off, and Adrian was incredibly grateful for it.

It wasn't as if Adrian was some sort of a criminal, or that he was on the run from an evil pack that were going to hunt him down like slavering beasts. That wasn't the deal.

It was more like he was invisible. Like he hadn't even actually ever been there. And when he'd walked away, no one even cared. So why make a big deal about it?

"I appreciate it. But there's honestly no pack. Not to write to or to talk to. I'm on my own."

Thomas frowned and shook his head. "Not anymore. My son's mate is part of our family, part of our pack, and I won't hear anything different."

Then, to Adrian's utter shock, Thomas pulled him into a huge bone-crushing hug. It was weird and sweet and dear.

Adrian just stood there, completely unsure of what to do.

It's okay. He won't hurt you. He's a good man and a great pack alpha. I can only hope that one day, I do as good a job.

Do you intend to take his place?

What? Do you think I'm going to leave it to Rian? Or Quin?

Adrian didn't say anything because...what was he supposed to say? Symon just didn't seem like the wolfiest of all possible wolves.

I know I'm more corporate than fuzzy, but I can do the job. There was an unshakable certainty in Symon's tone, and he had to grin. Wolfy wolf or not, Symon was an effortless alpha.

I trust you, was what he finally came out with.

Good. I love you.

His cheeks heated, and he was glad when Thomas let him go, because he dove back into Symon's arms, needing the contact.

Rian wandered in, blinking, hair standing up all over, his pajamas covered in little saguaro cactus prints. "Hey, Dad. Did you bring pastries?"

Thomas stared at Rian, face so serious. "Who are you?"

Rian wrinkled his nose. "Are you going senile, old man? Do you not recognize your middle son?"

"I thought you were some fancy-assed high-dollar lawyer type." Thomas pursed his lips. "You look like a ragamuffin."

"Ragamuffin? Definitely senile." Rian seemed unconcerned. "I was up all night playing grab ass with my brothers and this mountain lion."

"Is that what you call it?" Now it was Symon's dad's turn to look unimpressed. "I want to know why no one called me and let me know if there was a threat to the pack."

"Wasn't a threat to the pack," Rian announced. "It was a threat to money and business and possibly Symon's new mate. Have you met Adrian?"

"I've met Adrian. Adrian's part of the pack. The money, part of the pack. Business, part of the pack."

Symon shook his head. "Dad, it's not—"

"Are you part of the pack?"

"Well, I suppose, but I—"

"No. You're part of the pack. Ergo, all the rest of it's part of the pack. I'm the leader of the pack. I should have been notified."

Quin came in through the kitchen somehow, the huge box of pastries in one hand. A cruller—no, half of a cruller in the other. "Eh, you're here, aren't you? I guess you must have been notified. In fact, I called and said, yo, Dad."

Wait. Did Quin sleep in leather pants? Did he own anything that weren't leather pants? That had to get sweaty.

Ew.

Quin winked at Adrian as if he knew he was being stared at. "Want a doughnut?"

"Please." He wanted all the things. Sugar. Caffeine. For the earth to stop shifting under his feet.

Which might have worked, but then Isaac entered the room, kind of doing his slinky morning kitty walk. He looked all Pallas cat with his wide blinky eyes and morning hair. "Did I hear doughnuts? Whoa." Isaac jumped back when he saw Thomas, kind of crouching. If he had his tail, it would be lashing, Adrian thought. "Who are you?"

"Thomas Lukos. Symon's father. Pleased to meet you, erm..."

"Isaac." Isaac stared at the big guy as if he would bite.

"It's okay," Adrian told Isaac. "He's nice."

"If you say so." Isaac's eyes never left Thomas. "Are you sure I can have a doughnut?"

"Dad brought like eighty-four boxes of doughnuts, man." Quin tossed Isaac a doughnut, and he snatched it out of the air with reflexes that made them all blink.

Right.

Kitty.

It made sense.

"Well, eighty-four boxes should get us through at least ten a.m." Rian nodded. "Good choice."

"Yeah," Symon agreed. "We'll get Stan to make bacon sandwiches for everyone around noon, and then we can all decide whether or not we want to go out for Mexican."

Adrian considered whether or not to just have a meltdown. This was all a lot.

He gave Symon a hard stare. "Okay. So, we have a gunfight with a big cat. He is now in jail. Are we thinking that this whole thing is over? It really doesn't feel like 'let's have doughnuts and go out to eat Mexican food' over. Also, my apartment got burned down. And I don't even own a pair of socks now!"

"All right, the insurance has cut you a check." Rian started, and Adrian held one hand up.

"That's not the point, and I'm not finished. When is the office opening up? Is everybody at the office okay? What are we going to do about the code? What are we going to do about these back doors and how do we get rid of them? What do we do about the fact that there is another person out there who was obviously working with dickweed because he wasn't smart enough to do all of this by himself, solitary cat or no? When am I going to get to buy another pair of jeans? And what about my video games? And my couch. My couch is gone!"

Thomas stared at him for a second. "What happened to your apartment?"

"Oh, Jesus Christ." He stormed over to Quin and grabbed two doughnuts. "You said there were eighty-four boxes?"

"Eighty-three and a half now." Butter wouldn't melt in Quin's mouth.

"Do any of them have apple fritters in them?"

Thomas cleared his throat. "Yeah."

"Excellent, Isaac, let's go eat."

CHAPTER

FIFTEEN

By the time Symon and his brothers had explained everything to their dad, he was grumpy, tired, and overhyped on sugar.

Adrian and Isaac had been playing video games and then sprawled together, napping, so he got on his laptop and did what he did best.

Business.

He fired off emails to his legal team, cc'ing Rian on them. He wanted Carl kept in jail, no bail. He wanted the Henry guy found. He wanted to know who was paying Carl for the code.

Then he got a hold of the building manager at the office to have him sign off on getting everyone back to work. Security, he beefed up. And he called Helene about managing the rest of the team for him while he dealt with Adrian's life for a few days.

He caught himself sitting and growling.

He rarely growled, especially not at home, but he was definitely growling.

Symon wandered into the kitchen, just in case he was hungry, and Stan was standing there looking at him.

"What? What's the matter?"

"You sprung an ear, man."

Panicked, he reached up, finding nothing but his normal, human ears. He rolled his eyes at the tease and sort of smoothed his hair back, which, he had to admit, did seem a little shaggier than normal. "Ha ha, so funny."

Stan stared at him for a minute and then smiled. "You know that it's okay, right?"

"What?"

"You are a wolf, and that's okay."

Symon wasn't sure exactly what that was supposed to mean. He wasn't stupid. He understood that Stan was being comforting, but Symon had been there for Stan's attack.

Symon had seen what happened. Symon knew one had to control the wolf at all times because terrible things could happen.

To good people.

"I am a wolf," he admitted, "but—"

Stan shook his head, interrupting. "No. No buts. I've been thinking about this, and you are a wolf and a man. And you're a good man, but you're also a good wolf. Just like there are bad ones. Just like there are stupid ones and scared ones and wild ones and urbane ones. We are who we are. And denying any part of that can't help."

Symon stared at Stan. "What happened to you? Are you okay?"

"Yes. I'm absolutely fine." Stan chuckled at him, obviously tickled. "I like Adrian. I like him a lot. He's kind of a dork, but he's a wolf too. A wolf whose best friend is a kitty." Symon got a long, kind of judging look. "You and I have spent a lot of energy trying to be super Zen. Have you ever noticed how goddamn stressful it is?"

"I—" His mouth just kept falling open as he tried to talk. "I mean, yes. I just don't want to be what everyone thinks we are."

"So don't be. But don't deny half of yourself, either. I mean, is your dad a slavering beast?"

"No." No, his father was the definition of a good alpha. Controlled, but in touch with the wolf so he could lead the pack.

"So what's the hang-up? Is it me?" Stan tilted his head. "Because while I appreciate you and our relationship and our friendship, at some point you are going to have to lead the pack."

He knew. He wasn't sure how he was going to handle it, but he knew.

"And what are you going to do?" Symon asked.

"I'm going to come with you. I'm going to cook. I'm going to be Adrian's friend. I will probably play with your children."

"Aren't you interested in finding a mate?" It seemed to Symon that everyone deserved to feel as wonderful as he felt right now.

"No. I have a good life. I'm happy. I have my books. I have my kitchen. I have television. I have games and time with you in the pool. I have long walks in the mountains. And I'm safe here with you, and that's what I want."

Symon didn't know what to say, but he supposed it really wasn't his place to say anything. So he nodded. "You will always have a place in my home. In our home. No matter what."

"Fair enough. That's all I ask for. Is a place to live my life. The way I'd like to."

"And the periodic box of really, really good chocolate," Symon pointed out with a wink. He knew Stan's weaknesses.

"Yep. That's one of the advantages of being a turned werewolf." Stan chuckled. "It doesn't make me queasy like it does you."

"I still like it." He sighed. "You're right. I need to— You know what? I'm going to see if Adrian wants to go for a run with me."

"Take your brothers and Cy. Just in case. And that way he can get to know the pack."

"Good idea." He hugged Stan. "Thank you." Symon padded into the living room to wake his mate.

Adrian blinked up at him. *What? What's wrong?*

Nothing. I thought I'd ask if you wanted to go for a run.

A run? Like...put on your tennis shoes and jog? Because, yeah, no. Poor Adrian looked utterly confused.

No, baby. Wolf out and run. I have some land. I thought I'd see if the brothers wanted to go. Maybe Cy. He waited for the inevitable shock. Hell, Symon was a little shocked himself.

"Oh." Adrian actually said that out loud. *I've—I haven't run with the pack. Not since I was a kid. I'm not a very beautiful wolf.*

Yes, you are. It didn't matter to Symon that he hadn't seen Adrian. Adrian could shift and be pink and purple with three legs, one ear, jiggety teeth, and a lazy eye.

And Symon wouldn't give a shit.

He would know, his mate was beautiful.

Adrian rolled his eyes and opened his mouth to argue, and Symon just tugged him again. *Come on, let's go play. What do you have to lose?*

Goddess knew he wasn't on the table for that question.

All right, all right, I'll go. Don't let anybody bite me.

If anyone bites you but me, there will be hell to pay. Rules are rules.

Oh, look at you being all alpha wolfy and shit. It's kinda hot. Adrian gave him a nervous grin but stood, carefully extricating himself from Isaac's hug. *How do we do this? Do we go to the bedroom and get naked? And then meet them on the porch?* Adrian gave him a suspicious look. *Do you have a doggy door?*

I do not. Maybe Stan put one in. I never asked. He winked. Come on, baby. We'll go out my patio door. Let me call the heathens. He took Adrian's hand and led him to the private patio entrance he had, not the one off the family room. *Rian. Quin. Cy. Come run with me and Adrian. Wolf attire only.*

Coming, brother.

Yes, boss!

We're running? Rock on, bro!

The happiness from the guys made him bounce.

Should I ask dad?

He'll be hurt if you don't, Quin told him.

You want to go run, Dad? Symon asked.

He felt his dad's gentle humor. *Next time, son. Take your mate out without me this time.*

I will. Soon you'll go with him as well. He couldn't wait to see Adrian in his true form, in his wolf form.

Adrian raised an eyebrow.

"I was asking Dad. He said next time."

Adrian's relief was hard to miss.

"He's not a bad guy."

"Yeah, but you're all amazing. I'm...me."

"You're my mate. That's the most amazing thing in the world to me, baby." He took a hard kiss. "Now show me your wolf."

Adrian was nervous. Symon could see it in his eyes, but

his lover stripped down, baring himself before swallowing hard and closing his eyes.

He willed Adrian's wolf to come, to show for him, and slowly Adrian began to shift, the little wolf silvery and gray, eyes shining like the moon.

"Baby. You're beautiful." Adrian looked up at him, and he knew his wolf would say it better. So he shifted, letting his wolf come, and it was shocking, how easy it came.

Adrian bowed to him, muzzle on the ground. *Mate.*

Yes. My mate. He was glad he'd opened the patio door before he'd shifted. No doggie door. *So beautiful. Ready to go?*

He got a wide-eyed look. *Beautiful? You make me so happy...*

And you will make me happy for the rest of my life. He nuzzled at Adrian's ear. *Come on. See my territory.*

Your territory. Adrian smiled a wolfy, toothy grin. *Let's go.*

Rian and Quin joined them almost immediately, with Cy behind, watching their flanks as always. The big wolf was devoted to his pack, to the family, and having him there suited Symon to the ground.

They started to run, moving slowly at first as they headed up toward the mountain. As soon as they got deeper into the trees, deep enough to be able to play without any worries of seeing another human or even worse, being seen by one, they began to play.

Adrian was quick as lightning, slipping through the underbrush so easily that he could barely be seen. Symon imagined Adrian had had to learn to be stealthy early on. As pale as he was, he was like a shining beacon of oh, come shoot me.

On the other hand, he couldn't wait to see Adrian in the snow. His mate would simply disappear.

Regardless, it was Adrian who caught the first rabbit, snapping it up without it even so much as getting out a scream.

And then Adrian brought it to him. Offering the tribute with a deep bow and a happy tail.

He nipped it carefully, offering Adrian the most tender parts. Symon expected to feel appalled that they were hunting, expected his Zen human self to be disgusted.

That didn't happen. Wolves hunted. That was what they did. It was as natural as breathing.

And his mate honored him.

He'd never felt anything quite like this. Perhaps later it would confuse him, but right now it made perfect sense.

His mate was here. Loving him. Honoring him. Feeding him. And now he would do the same.

They took off, dancing and hunting, chasing tails and singing to the sky.

Three big red wolves, one gigantic gray wolf, and a tiny white wolf explored and hunted.

He'd hunted with his brothers for years, even if it had been a while, and it was so easy to fall back into familiar patterns. To allow Quin to flush out the prey. For Cy and Rian to take either side, and for him to go in for the kill.

Now they had Adrian to fill in all the blanks. To add to those places that they didn't have each other. He was clever and quicksilver, just the most nimble little wolf he'd ever seen.

By the time they returned to the house, he was panting, and they found the water feature he'd set up in the yard just for this reason, drinking deep. Stan let them in, smiling at them as they all filed into the family room, flopping together in a pile of ears and tails.

Adrian came right to him. Grooming his whiskers, smoothing the fur on his face. Nuzzling his ears, making sure every hair was perfectly in place.

It was adorable, especially considering that Adrian, the man, was not the most...fastidious on earth.

Are you well, mate? he asked, and Adrian chuffed softly.

I have a pack. There was a satisfaction in the sound of the wolf that he had never heard in Adrian's thoughts before.

You do. You're not alone. Not anymore.

And neither was he.

He stretched out long, encouraging Adrian to curl up into his side to rest, muzzle on Quin's flank.

Adrian wasn't alone, and neither was he.

He had his pack, and he was ready to run, live with his mate, start his family.

As soon as he caught the sons of bitches that were trying take down his company, at least...

End

WANT MORE?

Join the Spurs and Shifters Newsletter for free stories, news, and contests from Minerva Howe!

Or check out my Patreon for exclusive news and stories!

AFTERWORD

Waves Madly!

Thanks so much for reading my book! I'm so glad you made it to The End. If you liked the story, I hope you'll ponder leaving a rating at the retailer of your choice or adding a rec at Goodreads or BookBub!

Also, Minerva has her own Facebook page if you want to go like it, and I share a group with my other pseudonym, Julia Talbot!

Page: https://www.facebook.com/Minerva-Howe-102698554851288

Group: https://www.facebook.com/groups/juliatalbot

Get Spanky, y'all!

Minerva Howe

Also by Minerva Howe

Dragon Veil Universe

Dragon Hoard

Dragon Scholar

Dragon Collector

Dragon Treasure

Dragon Prophecy

Mist Dragon

Cloud Dragon

Shadow Dragon

Dragon Sanctuary

Winter Dragon

Ice Dragon

Frost Dragon

Snow Dragon

Frozen Dragon

Misunderstood

Wolven Winter

Shifting Winter

Healing Winter

Solitary Dragons

Archer

Aiden

Devlin

❧

Heartstone Rescue

Mending the Dragon's Heart

Healing the Dragon's Heart

Catching the Dragon's Heart

Forging the Dragon's Heart *standalone novella*

❧

Mated at the North Pole

Rudolph

❧

Mated to His Reindeer

Love at Frost Bite: Cupid

❧

Moonlight Mountain

Chosen Wolf

Found Vampire

Broken Wolf

❧

Planet Fantasy

Completely Alien

Space Pirate Playtoy

⁂

Rocky Mountain Java

Coffee and Honeybuns

Decaf and Bearclaws

⁂

Secret Springs Universe

Home for...

Home for Ryan

Home for Stone

Home for Charlie

Secrets Springs

Pens and Needles

Halos and Heroes

Fire and Ice

Pride and Power

History and Haunting

Secrets Springs Healing Hands

Bad Boy and a Baby

⁂

Oro Escondido

The Billionaire Dragon's Sweet Mate

Alpha Triplets

Hunter's Moon

Thunder Moon

Wolf Moon

Alpha Triplets Box Set

Dragon Triplets

Dragon of Fire

Dragon of Glass

Dragon of Passion

Gryphon Triplets

The Gryphon's Jewel

The Gryphon's Prize

The Gryphon's Dragon

ABOUT THE AUTHOR

Minerva Howe is the kinky alter-ego of Julia Talbot. She lives in the great Southwest, where there is hot and cold running rodeo, cowboys, and everything from meat and potatoes to the best Tex-Mex. A full-time author, Minerva is a hybrid author. She believes that everyone deserves a happy ending, so she writes about love without limits, where boys love boys, girls love girls, and boys and girls get together to get wild, especially when her crazy paranormal characters are involved. Visit Minerva's website at: minervahowe.com

9 798869 397553